**NEW YORK REVIEW BOO**
CLASSICS

# SLOW DAYS, FAST COMPANY

EVE BABITZ is the author of several books of fiction, including *Sex and Rage: Advice to Young Ladies Eager for a Good Time*, *L.A. Woman*, and *Black Swans: Stories*. Her nonfiction works include *Fiorucci, the Book* and *Two by Two: Tango, Two-Step, and the L.A. Night*. She has written for publications including *Ms.* and *Esquire* and in the late 1960s designed album covers for the Byrds, Buffalo Springfield, and Linda Ronstadt. Her novel *Eve's Hollywood* is published by NYRB Classics.

MATTHEW SPECKTOR is the author of the novels *American Dream Machine* and *That Summertime Sound*, as well as a nonfiction book of film criticism. He is a founding editor of the *Los Angeles Review of Books*.

# SLOW DAYS, FAST COMPANY

*The World, the Flesh, and L.A.*

**EVE BABITZ**

*Introduction by*
**MATTHEW SPECKTOR**

NEW YORK REVIEW BOOKS

*New York*

THIS IS A NEW YORK REVIEW BOOK
PUBLISHED BY THE NEW YORK REVIEW OF BOOKS
207 East 32nd Street, New York, NY 10016
www.nyrb.com

Frontispiece and concluding photographs of the author by Annie Leibovitz
© Annie Leibovitz/(Contact Press Images)

Library of Congress Cataloging-in-Publication Data
Babitz, Eve.
 Eve's Hollywood / Eve Babitz ; introduction by Holly Brubach.
    pages cm — (New York Review Books classics)
 ISBN 978-1-59017-890-4 (paperback)
 1. Single women—Fiction. 2. Hollywood (Los Angeles, Calif.)—Fiction.
 I. Title.
 PS3552.A244E84 2015
 813'.54—dc23

                    2015017144


ISBN 978-1-59017-890-4
Available as an electronic book; ISBN 978-1-59017-891-1

Printed in the United States of America on acid-free paper.
20  19  18  17  16  15  14  13

# CONTENTS

# INTRODUCTION

ANY WRITER may be in or out of step with his or her time, but a
great one is inextricably bound to place. Whether native or in exile,
certain writers have a tone and temper in their work that is so
conditioned by and suffused with the locus of their creation that it
becomes almost impossible to consider these things separately. Such
is the case with Eve Babitz, whose novels are richly Californian, not
just in their regional particulars—I can think of no cultural artifact
of any kind that better preserves Sunset Boulevard, circa 1974, than
*Slow Days, Fast Company*—but also in their method and in their
mood. This is a strength, naturally: Babitz's Los Angeles is as
idiosyncratically true as William Faulkner's Mississippi, and as
distinct from that place as it is from Joan Didion's L.A., with which
it nevertheless overlaps. Still, there is sometimes an irritating
tendency, one as sexist as it is parochial, to imagine Babitz's work as
an accidental, perhaps even unimportant byproduct of her glamorous biography. I am loath to bring it up. Babitz attended Hollywood
High. Her godfather was Igor Stravinsky. At twenty, she was
famously photographed playing chess in the nude with Marcel
Duchamp. (Only she, alas, is nude. The artist was dressed.) After
that—well, to start laying out the names of Babitz's paramours is to
begin building the wall that obscures our view of her work. Even if
the famous names factor into the work, which they do—Babitz's
books are nothing if not gossipy—is it important to our understanding that one of her lovers was, say, the lead singer of a famous sixties
rock band who died in a bathtub in Paris, or that another went on to
star in an even more famous trilogy of science-fiction movies, and so

on? Kind of. But the moment those names are named (in *Slow Days, Fast Company* they're largely pseudonymous, or brushed aside in a way that feels aptly dishabille), Babitz ceases to be the heroine of her own literary biography; she becomes just another flytrap, a not quite cautionary tale, a party girl spattered with genius instead of (this distinction seems important) an actual genius who just happened to, y'know, like to party. Of which, so what? The twentieth century is littered with fabled *male* geniuses who enjoyed their opium, their reefer, their booze and sex and cocaine, but very seldom are these particular titans introduced drugs and conquests first.

"You can't write a story about L.A. that doesn't turn around in the middle or get lost," Babitz remarks at the very beginning of *Slow Days, Fast Company*, a statement that seems on the one hand the sort of gnomic pronouncement that books about Los Angeles tend to invoke (see also the famous first sentence of Bret Easton Ellis's *Less Than Zero*) but on the other a very deliberate statement of an aesthetic and an intent. A few pages later, she notes:

> *I* can't get a thread to go through to the end and make a straightforward novel. *I* can't keep everything in my lap, or stop rising flurries of sudden blind meaning. But perhaps if the details are all put together, a certain pulse and sense of place will emerge, and the integrity of empty space with occasional figures in the landscape can be understood at leisure and in full....

Aside from being a superb articulation of both process and approach (how Babitz excels at those "rising flurries of sudden blind meaning"), this passage is telling in other ways. Babitz knows all about what she terms "a straightforward novel"; there are nearly as many informed remarks about Marcel Proust, Virginia Woolf, and Henry James in these pages as there are about parties and pharmaceuticals, and in fact her sense of form and narrative construction is no more casual or attenuated than that of her approximate historical peers (never mind Didion or Renata Adler—the work is more shapely than, say, Kurt Vonnegut or Richard Brautigan, neither of whom ever apologized for wayward novelistic construction). But that reference to "the integrity of empty space" and "occasional figures in the landscape" is also worth noting. Babitz was, initially, an artist—she designed album covers for Atlantic Records in the sixties, most famously for Buffalo Springfield and the Byrds—and so a certain painterly sense races through this book as well, a nervous preoccupation (as West Coast artists are given to have) with light.

> The women moved easily around the patio and spacious backyard, holding drinks, seeming mildly amused at the oval stomachs draped in flowered cotton fabric. Their wedding rings reflected the pink twilight, their golden bracelets caught the light of the mustard hills.

> But outside the afternoon was lethal: No sunglasses could cut the glare, and even your pores shrank back against the light.

Babitz's descriptive knack would be reason enough to recommend *Slow Days, Fast Company*—the first passage quoted above is a Renoir in two sentences—but it's her ferocious aphoristic intelligence that finally steals the show. The book is arranged geographically, and at times meteorologically. Each chapter describes either a particular location (Bakersfield, Palm Springs, Laguna Beach—like any good Angeleno, Babitz is forever in flight from the city; like any strong writer, she is endlessly kicking against her region's bitter complexities) or a weather event: rain or Santa Anas. Where Didion and Raymond Chandler found the latter apocalyptic, Babitz greets them with exultancy:

> Once, when I was fifteen, I walked for an entire afternoon along the empty cement in 110 degrees of hot dry winds just to get the feel of them, alone. Everyone else was hiding inside.
> I know those winds the way Eskimos know their snows.

That exuberance I'll return to in a moment—it seems a particularly vexed quality, at least in its relation to the more Calvinistic aspects of the American grain—but what really sets *Slow Days, Fast Company* apart is the strength and radical compression of its thought. Avowedly a love story, addressed to an unnamed male companion, the book follows Babitz from one ambivalent attachment to another, through an erotic entanglement with a gay man named Shawn, multiple threesomes, evenings of Quaaludes and cocaine, and various bygone L.A. establishments—Ports, The Luau, Hamburger Hamlet—make their appearances. Yet whatever orgiastic qualities are suggested within the narrative (which is never particularly graphic), it is Babitz's observational skill, her wisdom, for want of a better word, that one remembers. "I did not become famous but I got near enough to smell the stench of success. It smelt like burnt cloth and rancid gardenias, and I realized that the truly awful thing about success is that it's held up all those years as the thing that would make everything all right," she writes; elsewhere, with a sharpness that still takes my breath away, "All art fades but sex fades fastest." Even when she is merely describing a style or a gesture, she will occasionally elide this into something close to metaphysics: "The way he drove a car was the most inexplicable thing about him; he drove with an absent-minded, almost puttering kindliness, as though when he was inside a car, the world got slower; it was time for reverie almost." To imagine writing this vivid and alert could be tossed off, savant-like, by some hungover glamour queen still lolling on soiled sheets at the Chateau Marmont—even if, as the book itself practically suggests, this happens to have been the case—remains an insult to writing itself, let alone to the writer in question.

It's worth considering *why* Babitz's work stands now to be remembered, instead of never having faded from view in the first place. The unabashedly hedonistic qualities of *Slow Days, Fast Company*—and of Babitz's other books, which are hardly less so—are difficult, I think, for some critics to properly apprehend. There's consequence, but no punishment involved here. If Babitz's close geographic and topical peer Didion—"peer" insofar as Didion, too, knew and could describe the nightly denizens of Chasen's restaurant, say—has already been canonized, I'd argue it's because of the stern, outsiderish judgment she leveled upon the scene. Sternness was inimical to Babitz, and she knew it. In the long and slightly loopy acknowledgments section that precedes *Eve's Hollywood*, she thanks "the Didion-Dunnes for having to be who I'm not." To this day, I think, there remains a suspicion of California, and of its artists, as if an embrace of gentle weather and open geography is tantamount to a lack of rigor. Pity, but of course this goes back a few hundred years, at least, and if we can't rewind a nation's drab and crippling Protestantism, we, those of us who have the pleasure now of reading and rereading Eve Babitz, can bask in the joy and infectious energy of her sensibility. The author herself says it best, in a passage where she shrugs off her own embarrassment over loving L.A., describing the happiness she feels stepping off an airplane: "My claustrophobia from San Francisco begins to vanish—that cheerful shipshape vitality of the north violates my spirit and I long for vast sprawls, smog, and luke nights: L.A. It is where I work best, where I can live, oblivious to physical reality." Yeah. That obliviousness is worth noting too. Who needs physical reality when you can gambol, instead, in expansive space, in sunlight, uncertainty, and in the moment, which is to say—in eternity?

—MATTHEW SPECKTOR

# SLOW DAYS,
# FAST COMPANY

THIS IS a love story and I apologize; it was inadvertent. But I want it clearly understood from the start that I don't expect it to turn out well. I'm not going to give you an "although I am wry and world-weary, me and Sam have found the answer together which only *we* share and *you* can't come in except to press your nose against this book." It's bad luck for one thing. I know this lady who just made a fortune writing about her uplifting redemption, practically, from Falling In Love, and while she was on tour promoting the paperback the light of her heart ran into the night and disappeared off the face of the earth. Besides its being bad luck to even whisper that you're happy, it's also not nice basically. I mean, Scott and Zelda really weren't very nice bragging up and down Fifth Avenue about how perfect everything was. But the real truth has nothing to do with bad luck or niceness; the real truth is that I've never known any man-woman thing to pan out (it may pan out to them, of course, but couples in middle age who don't speak to each other are not my idea of a good movie).

I have a lot of friends who are positive life isn't worth living without True Love Forever. They're always on the prowl and sulk against the gods when they go to a party and don't fall in love. Women, especially, engage themselves in ghastly self-inflicted tortures for which they've been primed since childhood. After all, historically it's always been dreadful for women, and the logic given them was "It's going to be dreadful so you may as well learn to enjoy it."

I talked to my friend Graham the other day and told him that perhaps it'd be better to forgo men altogether and take up with women, only I had a horrible suspicion that I'd wind up in the same heartbreak hotel as I did with men. "No you won't," he reasoned. "*You* be the man and that way *you* get to be the shit." I had a sudden transplant of sense as I imagined myself "the man" and just how creepy I bet I could be: dodging emotional entanglements and lying and otherwise having a lovely time. Forgetting to phone.

Since it's impossible to get this one I'm in love with to read anything unless it's about or to him, I'm going to riddle this book with Easter Egg italics so that this time it won't take him two and a half years to read my book like it did the first one. The seduction of a non-reader is how I plan to tie up L.A.

Virginia Woolf said that people read fiction the same way they listen to gossip, so if you're reading this at all then you might as well read my private asides written so he'll read it. I have to be extremely funny and wonderful around him just to get his attention at all and it's a shame to let it all go for one person.

# SLOW DAYS

*Darling:*
  *I know you don't care about the art of the novel but you might like the part about Forest Lawn.*

IT'S WELL known that for something to be fiction it must move right along and not meander among the bushes gazing into the next county. Unfortunately, with L.A. it's impossible. You can't write a story about L.A. that doesn't turn around in the middle or get lost. And since it's the custom for people who "like" L.A. to embrace everything wholesale and wallow in Forest Lawn, all the stories you read make you wonder why the writer doesn't just go ahead and jump, get it over with.

I love L.A. The only time I ever go to Forest Lawn is when someone dies. A kid from New York once said: "Look. Which would you rather? To spend eternity looking out over these pretty green hills or in some overcrowded ghetto cemetery next to the expressway in Queens?" L.A. didn't invent eternity. Forest Lawn is just an example of eternity carried to its logical conclusion. I love L.A. because it does things like that.

People nowadays get upset at the idea of being in love with a city, especially Los Angeles. People think you should be in love with other people or your work or justice. I've been in love with people and ideas in several cities and learned that the lovers I've loved and the ideas I've embraced depended on where I was, how cold it was, and what I had to do to be able to stand it. It's very easy to stand L.A., which is why it's almost inevitable that all sorts of ideas get entertained, to say nothing of lovers. Logical sequence, however, gets lost in the shuffle. Art is supposed to uphold standards of organization and structure, but you can't have those things in Southern California—people have tried. It's difficult to be truly serious when you're in a city that can't even put up a skyscraper for fear the earth will start up one day and bring the whole thing down around everyone's ears. And so the artists in Los Angeles just don't have that burning eagerness people expect. And they're just not *serious*. It makes friends of mine in New York pace and seethe just remembering the unreasoning delight one encounters with the cloudlike marvels of Larry Bell.

The idea of an "artistic community" evaporates into the slow days. Inspiration and words like that get hurried along with the fast company; it's impossible to tell if one's been inspired, or if it was the cocaine, or what. In an Italian café—where one day the incredibly beautiful young waitresses are going to poison (I hope) one by one all the vulgar and insulting men who've ever gotten away with murder and crude remarks—one night I saw on the wall, neatly, in black Magic Marker: "It ain't Hollywood, my boy, it's mescalito." In Los Angeles it's hard to tell if you're dealing with the real true illusion or the false one.

The houses and architecture that originated in Los Angeles are entitled the "bungalow" style. I live in one. A bungalow.

People with sound educations and good backgrounds get very pissed off in L.A. "*This* is not a city," they've always complained. "How dare you people call this place a city!"

They're right. Los Angeles isn't a city. It's a gigantic, sprawling, ongoing studio. Everything is off the record. People don't have time to apologize for its not being a city when their civilized friends suspect them of losing track of the point.

When I was growing up, civilized friends of my parents' and even my parents used to complain all the time about how the L.A. County Art Museum was a travesty unparalleled anywhere for dopiness. They'd really get angry each time they recalled how Stravinsky was never so much as nodded to by "the city." I used to wonder, when I was little, how a city nodded to Stravinsky. City Hall was all the way downtown and Stravinsky lived in West Hollywood. These adults used to sigh and say, "If he lived anywhere else ... *any*where else, they would have done something about him. But not Los Angeles." I think that the truth was that Stravinsky lived in L.A. because when you're in your studio, you don't have to be a finished product all the time or make formal pronouncements. Work and love—the two best things—flourish in studios. It's when you have to go outside and define everything that they often disappear.

In the View section of the *L.A. Times* every now and then, you'll read about some doctor or lawyer who says, "My wife, Shirley, and I have thought it over and we've decided to retire from success and try failure for a few years. We feel the variety will enlarge us." I *know* L.A. is the only place on earth where people do that.

When the Ferus Gallery began exposing the rest of the country to Los Angeles art in the fifties, New York art people quickly observed that everyone seemed to be obsessed with perfection in L.A. The frames had to be perfect—the backs of the frames, even. "The Finish Fetish" it was called. Like the Beach Boys of that same mode when all that harmony fell out of the sky in seamless clouds. Rock and roll in L.A. tries even now *not* to be so gorgeous, to be raunchy and soulful, but it won't work. Linda Ronstadt and The Eagles and Jackson Browne can't scare anyone. Like the art from the old Ferus, L.A. rock and roll is just such perfection.

No one likes to be confronted with a bunch of disparate details that God only knows what they mean. *I* can't get a thread to go through to the end and make a straightforward novel. *I* can't keep everything in my lap, or stop rising flurries of sudden blind meaning. But perhaps if the details are all put together, a certain pulse and sense of place will emerge, and the integrity of empty space with occasional figures in the landscape can be understood at leisure and in full, no matter how fast the company.

# BAKERSFIELD

*What I want to do is, one Saturday, we'll wrap all our troubles in dreams and get in the car (you drive), and I'll take you on my glorious Weekend in the wilds of Kern County.*

*The first thing we do when we get to Bakersfield is we check into the "World's Oldest Motel," the Bakersfield Inn, which sometimes looks even better than the Beverly Hills Hotel. But cheaper. You can get a gigantic room with two queen-size beds and a dueña room in the front where you enter, so someone can stay up and drink and watch TV while the other person sleeps—anyway, there's Neutrogena in the shower—and it only costs fifteen dollars a night. There are two pools and lots of those tall skinny palm trees, and Bakersfield has a smog problem so that sunsets around there are just heaven.*

*When night falls we'll go to a Basque restaurant, stuff ourselves, and go dancing at The Blackboard. And in the morning we'll have brunch at the Bakersfield Inn, where tons of biscuits and gravy and chicken and scrambled eggs and bacon and just everything including champagne is only about five dollars. We'll have fun.*

IT WAS one of those blazing L.A. days when everything seems about to lose its sense of gravity and just rise from the sidewalks, when I received my first fan letter from a Frank D. He was writing, he said, from a small room in London and outside his window a crowd had gathered because a bomb had exploded in a car, outside where it was damp and cold. He had gone to England to teach school, he said, but he was from Bakersfield, California, and he had grown up between there and a beach town south of Los Angeles. When people in London asked him what it was like in California, he added, he pointed to his wall where a piece I'd written was pinned up because, he said, it explained California much better than he could.

I was a little amazed that one of my sultry glimpses of this coast could inspire someone (who obviously wasn't a ne'er-do-well) to write me a fan letter. He told me about seeing Beckett plays in London, about Welsh girls and married men, about the children he tried to teach.

We wrote back and forth for almost six months. The contrast between his existence during the poverty-stricken English winter and my own L.A. days of champagne cocktails and diets made me realize that the world wasn't *all* power struggles between me and pasta. In the back of my mind I thought, Anytime I want, I can forsake this dinner party and jump into real life.

Then Frank D. wrote to tell me that he was coming back to California, and we arranged to meet on a certain night in Hollywood for dinner. He'd be coming in from Bakersfield (120 miles, most of them flat), he said, from his father's ranch. His father grew grapes, he added, and I asked Frank to bring me some.

Frank D. arrived, and he was not short (I'd been afraid he'd be short for some reason, maybe because he taught small children). He was tall, in fact, lankily graceful, and smart. He referred to people as "folks" even though he was only twenty-five years old, and he had a sort of innate kindness polished over by such good manners that he seemed to have stepped right out of a Leslie Howard impersonation. If in *Petrified Forest* Bette Davis and Leslie Howard had got married and lived ever after in that truck stop, Frank D. would have been their son.

He brought with him a twenty-four-pound box of grapes—three different kinds of grapes: Thompson seedless (those green ones), Exotics (those almost-black ones), and Cardinals (those dark rose-colored ones). On the outside of the box was one of the beautiful California labels usually found on orange crates; the label had his father's name on it, below the picture of his vineyards.

"Jesus!" I said, looking at the box. "*These* are the grapes you grow?"

Their stems were strong and green, not brown and brittle like in the store, and they hung perfectly like a still life, no matter which way they were turned. Frank D. was amused that I would find grapes so exciting—but I had never before seen a whole crate of fruit, brand new, packed just for me.

I had almost bought some grapes earlier in the year, but they cost $1.40 for a tiny bunch, and it occurred to me that I'd probably never eat grapes again. First I'd abandoned them for Chavez, and now that the unions had won, grapes were out of my income bracket. I asked if the ones he had brought me were Union grapes and he told me they'd been picked by the Teamsters.

My immediate hunch was that the Teamsters management stepped in, after Chavez did all the work, and skimmed off the cream. Chavez, after all, was the first man to be able to organize farm labor and it didn't seem fair. (Maybe the Teamsters seemed more American to the farm workers than Chavez did with his

Gandhian fasts and no money. Maybe if he'd got himself a nice house with a pool and air conditioning, they would have stayed with him. And maybe their leader—who seems so glamorous to me—seemed like a naïf to them for not using his power to get a limousine. If I were a unionized farm laborer and paying dues, I'd like to know that my leader was every bit as scary as the boss and not some vulnerable saint.)

"I had friends when I went away to school who even used to pick the grapes out of their fruit cocktails," Frank told me. He laughed and since I'd never known anyone young who was not for Chavez, and couldn't imagine anyone who wouldn't be, I naturally assumed Frank was automatically on the side of progress and the path of righteousness, even if his father was not.

I also took it for granted that any person my age or younger would leave Bakersfield the minute he could if he were not emotionally retarded. I'd passed through the town all my life going to San Francisco and it was a place that was so hot and listless and without character, so flat that mirages of water on the road appeared closer than they did anywhere else I'd ever been. How could a young person want to stay there? It was beyond the realm of possibility.

Frank had gone away to school and stayed away, even going to England to get away from the valley. And since I've always lived in cities where a lot of the people are desperate refugees from small towns determined never to go back except for funerals, I thought everyone was like that. I couldn't imagine someone in this age remaining past twenty years old outside of New York, Los Angeles, or London. Especially in Bakersfield.

The only thing good, in fact, that I'd ever heard about Bakersfield was that there were some nice Basque restaurants there. These restaurants, it was said, were wonderful because everyone sat at long tables and the food that was served was untoward in its variety, mass, and goodness. My parents had told me of the twenty-course lunch they had found for two dollars, and other people had confirmed the existence of these fabulous cheap feasts.

In Los Angeles, Frank and I went out to dinner (three courses, eight dollars per person), and because I always go to the same restaurant, we brought about ten pounds of grapes for the proprietor; he stood back, wide-eyed, as I presented a giant basket in luscious splendor.

"Where'd these come from?" he wondered.

Frank explained about the vineyard, and my proprietor friend asked about wine. (All we ever think about, really, me and my friends, is wine.) "Wine grapes are different," Frank said. "They're not like table grapes. Wine grapes are the grapes no one wants, so it doesn't matter what they look like."

The proprietor brought us a bottle of wine anyway, thinking we'd want some. Which we did. So Frank and I drank, and although he was determined to find out all about me (like how I write and how I came to write), I changed the subject to the vineyards, and pushed it so that soon he was telling me that if I really wanted to know what it was like, I should come to Bakersfield and see for myself.

Not having expected things to go so far, I nearly refused, because Bakersfield had never been my idea of a destination. But romantic notions of valley ranchers danced in my head and I told him I'd go on the following weekend.

The next morning I woke up and thought I'd been crazy, but by that time it was too late. Frank had already begun doing things like making plane reservations and sending telegrams. I didn't want to be stuck up there with no car so I skittishly decided to drive, although I'm terrified of out-of-town freeways and those huge fruit trucks that suck up little VW's like mine into their vacuums.

Somehow, though, as the weekend approached, I began to look forward to the adventure—which would surely be unlike anything I'd ever experienced.


It takes two hours for an ordinary person to get from Hollywood to Bakersfield, so I planned on three, and got out of the house and onto the Hollywood Freeway by 7:00 a.m. At 10:00 a.m., I found the Lamont turnoff, which leads to Mr. D.'s vineyard, a few miles south of Bakersfield. There was a café on the Lamont turnoff—a red clapboard house with eucalyptus trees around it and orange groves after that, and trucks were parked in front. Pie, I thought, I bet they have real pie there. And real hamburgers that they make themselves, and maybe even real lemonade. But pie was my main thought.

Frank said he'd be working until twelve packing grapes into those giant fruit trucks. He'd be in the shed, he told me.

The "shed" was an L-shaped building about half a block long where refrigerated rooms stored grapes piled high to the high ceiling. In every direction lay the flat valley surrounded by foothills on the south, west, and east and going on forever to the north.

I found Frank wheeling a ten-foot-high stack of grapes in wooden boxes to the back of a truck, and he told me that I'd be taken around the ranch by one of the foremen over at another vineyard and that he, Frank, would drive me there. Most of the ranchers, I noticed that day, drove mustard-gold Fords or Buicks—gold because dust didn't show on that color. The men all had two-way radios in their cars, too, which they took to like toy trains. If they could have said "Roger, over and out" without feeling too dumb, they would have.

We passed one vineyard on the way that wasn't like the others I'd seen. It was full of weeds, of carelessness.

"Those are wine grapes," Frank said. "They don't matter."

"How come?"

"Because all they do with those is pick them and send them to the winery."

We found Sam, my guide, five miles away, at another vineyard which had sleeping quarters. Beside the bunkhouse was a row of wooden cages, each about four feet square, all huddled together, some on top of each other. Inside the cages were roosters with their combs and wattles cut off. The kind of roosters they use for cockfights.

"Do they have cockfights here?" I asked Sam as Frank drove away.

"Yeah, those Filipinos, that's all they live for...gambling, any kind of thing they can gamble about. The sheriff was over here this last Sunday and we've tried to make them stop but we just can't."

Sam lives two lives. In the summer he works on the ranch and is in charge of various crews picking the crops. In the winter he teaches and coaches the football team in one of the Bakersfield schools. He looks like a Marlboro commercial up close. And he treated me with a chivalrous masculine know-how that I sopped up like a person who'd never heard of how chivalry was just another nefarious masculine scheme to keep women in their place. During the whole time I was in Bakersfield, in fact, the only swear word I heard was "hell," and I didn't hear one single anatomical crudity or obscenity, or see one double-entendre smirk shooting back and forth among the men when a woman walked into the room. I got the feeling that these men take liberties only if they want to be shot by outraged brothers or husbands. It may not be the best way to do things, but it does make for a pleasant weekend.

The other two things I didn't see in Bakersfield were (a) platform shoes—I suspect men really can't stand platform shoes—and (b) diet colas.

Sam drove me around and showed me various groups of pickers. There were Mexicans, Arabs, Filipinos, and Puerto Ricans—both men and women. All make $2.50 an hour and twenty-five cents a box—except for the local high school guys who just make $2.50 an hour.

The Chavistas were picketing some of the fields we passed, taunting the workers who'd gone into the Teamsters Union instead of sticking with Chavez. The situation was touchy and I was told that violence was common—but while I was there it was so hot and humid I don't see how anyone could have gotten it together to start a fight. The night before I arrived, it had rained and the humidity was terrible, but with the 4/60 air conditioning it wasn't too bad. ("Four/sixty is when you have four windows open going sixty miles an hour," Frank had informed me.)

Sam began telling me more about grapes than anyone could possibly want to know, but I got to understand why Frank's father was considered one of the most respected growers in the valley. Even I could tell that in the row after row of grapevines, the grapes grew bigger, fell more beautifully on their stems, and tasted better than any grapes I'd ever seen before. The rows were spotlessly clean, manicured like Beverly Hills.

Grapevines, for the first two years, do not produce anything sellable. By the third year they produce well enough for the grapes to be sent to a winery. Only in the fourth year does a vine become commercial. The grapes begin in flowered clusters which, if left alone, will sally forth with tiny little tight bunches good for nothing. So the flowers are stripped down so fewer grapes will grow. ("This year," Frank told me, "we used little hairbrushes. They work.") By the time the grapes begin to grow they are again trimmed down to the point where they are called "five-shouldered," which means five main branches off the main stem in each cluster. Meanwhile, the whole grapevine itself has to be thrown over a support stick so the hot sun won't dry up the grapes.

The best of these immaculately tended grapes are sold under one label. The best grapes this year are gorgeous, the same size, and their five shoulders fall languidly perfectly no matter how you pick them up.

The lesser grapes are sold under lesser labels by Frank's father, although some table-grape growers put all their grapes into one label, shipping any old thing. These growers' products are referred to as "garbage" by men like Frank's father.

I asked Sam if he was proud to work for Mr. D., and he said, "There aren't too many men like him around anymore, you know. He doesn't just grow grapes, he really makes sure they are the best, and he knows what he's doing. These other growers get in here, they don't care, they ship them off to the winery—what do they care?"

We passed a bunch of Chavistas who yelled out at him, and he growled something inaudible and bristled. Mr. D. was one of the first twelve growers in the valley to sign with Chavez. That, of course, was before the Teamsters came and offered him a "sweetheart" contract—which is why the Chavistas are so mad. But the growers know, Frank thought, that in three years the Teamsters too will get tough and there will be no more sweetheart contracts.

We came to a field where women were picking grapes and their field forewoman was a local Chicana named Louise who stood out in that humid sun wearing ice-blue eye shadow and nice thick fake eyelashes. The other women wore hats and scarves to shield their faces from getting tan and I thought about the PABA cream I had with me, which Adele Davis guaranteed would protect me from the sun (as did *Vogue)*. I thought about telling Louise, but...

Back at the shed, I was introduced to Mr. D., who looked at me with puzzled care and the eyes of "And what are you doing with my son?" In his repertoire there were no young women who just drove up to Bakersfield simply to see what they could see and there were also no strangers brought home by his children, especially from L.A. L.A. was a foreign and not-easily-understood state of affairs. Why would anyone live there?

There was no reason I could give him for being in Bakersfield other than that I was a frivolous young woman prone to adventure—and his dignified posture was not about to get an explanation like that from me. He'd been up since 5:00 a.m. What *did* people do in Los Angeles, I began to wonder, besides rather useless business involving typewriters and offices? They didn't tend to essentials like growing food, that was for sure. They just breezed along in the supermarkets and went home to watch television, not knowing a thing about vineyards or orchards.

Frank finished loading his last crates into the truck. The heat was astounding.

"Come with me," Frank said. "The food's great here."

Near the shed was a small group of wooden houses, one an office and another a lunch place where each day at twelve a trio of American ladies served forth lunch for Mr. D. and his immediate circle (maybe twenty people). I realize now what an outsider I was, what an object of curiosity, though at the time I just sailed right in, not devoid of curiosity.

The table was long and the food was so American I hadn't tasted anything like it in I don't know how long. All these years of diets and yogurt, French cafés, Italian kitchens, Greek food ... This food was cooked for Americans who worked hard and liked their food simple. There were homemade biscuits, large squashes with cheese melted over the top, a salad of small tomatoes and Bermuda onions, green beans, lovely meatloaf, a pitcher of iced tea, another salad of cucumbers, and for dessert, pie. It was banana raisin cream pie, the very pie I'd been thinking of since I turned off the freeway.

Frank and I drove back to Bakersfield from Lamont in a dusty mustard-gold car against a dusty mustard-gold landscape of suede hills rolling against the markings of telephone poles linked with fine wires of black. The sky was heavy beyond Bear Mountain and the land gave up nothing but dry golden wild rye, and looked as it must have always looked.

We began to talk. Frank, unlike everyone I met in his milieu, had boundless energy and would talk even after working since dawn, and Frank seemed more worldly to me at first and he didn't seem to belong there. He reminded me of men I knew in New York who tried to be vegetarians and played recorder duets by Mozart, but then he looked at his hands, covered with blisters, and said, "I was out branding cattle last Sunday. I haven't roped cattle in years; look, my hands aren't used to it."

"Cattle?" I said. "You roped them?"

"I learned how a long time ago from this guy on the ranch," he told me.

"What do they all think of you going to London, the exact opposite of this?"

"They think, I guess, 'England? What do you *do* in England?'" He laughed. "They don't understand England at all."

"I don't understand it either," I said. And I didn't. There he was in England reading some American hip paper, coming across a piece of mine about L.A., writing to me. I felt luxuriously involved in an insolvable mystery, my favorite way to feel. I didn't really want to understand, preferring romance to sound reasoning. If he were to be like he was, there was nothing he could really tell me about himself that would ever match roping cattle, living in England, and being from this endless landscape of rolling gold, driving through in a golden car.

Mr. D.'s home was a large ranch-style house in a classy part of Bakersfield where all the lawns were green and flowers grew. There was a pool (which we swam in) and fruit trees in the backyard, but I hadn't been in a house so American for such a long time. Even my friends' parents in Los Angeles were more European, more integrated into New York and Paris, if only because of their children.

After we swam, we sat in a cool living room and talked and talked and talked. There was a party that night that Frank had been invited to—his first social event in the valley since returning from England, but really it had been longer than that, he told me, because most of these people he hadn't seen since high school or even grammar school.

"What kind of party will this be?" I asked, thinking, What shall I wear? I had gone one time into the square enclaves of Orange County with a friend of mine to his high school class's tenth reunion and I'd worn a violent red dress with a red hat and red shoes because he'd wanted to show all of them that he'd moved out of their understanding and into some flashy movie-land (which he had). But the fury in the eyes of the women prevented me from ever doing that again, and besides, I wanted to be spoken to without being bushwhacked in the ladies room (as had happened in Orange County). My mother had found a "decent outfit," as she called it, which she bestowed on me—a seersucker Mode O'Day (really, that's where it was from) skirt and top that couldn't hurt a fly. It was the only "decent outfit" I had, and some last-minute respect for the rightness of things made me bring it along. Of course I shall wear that, I decided.

"The girl whose house it's at went to grammar school with me," Frank explained. "She was the most beautiful girl in the fifth grade."

"Everyone will probably be adulterous," I remarked, thinking of the hot eyes that had fastened upon each other at the Orange County high school reunion, eyes of the past.

He laughed, Frank did, and he said, "Is that really how it'll be?"

Not a hint, of course, of anything like that. Not a whisper of sin, not a glimpse of passion by the men for women beyond their own wives, not a trace of a signal from the women beyond cheerful interest in each other's children. Of the forty or so people there, all between twenty-five and thirty-three, ten were pregnant.

The women moved easily around the patio and spacious backyard, holding drinks, seeming mildly amused at the oval stomachs draped in flowered cotton fabric. Their wedding rings reflected the pink twilight, their golden bracelets caught the light of the mustard hills. There was no extra energy in those women beyond their children or their particular geography. There was no energy for humor or wit, and I wondered at my friends in L.A. who were always brimming over with spare words and bright phrases.

There are three main Basque restaurants in Bakersfield that I've heard of: The Nyreaga, The White Bear, and The Pyrénées. The Nyreaga is the most famous because you have to get there between 6:30 and 6:45 in order to get dinner and people descend upon the tables in one fell swoop. The forty of us from the party went to The White Bear and thirty-nine of us were prepared for what happened next. I was not. There was pickled tongue, soup with bowls of beans and hot sauce on the side, bread, wine, spaghetti, string beans, fried chicken, roast beef, kidneys and mushrooms, baked fish, french fries, a salad, a sort of fabulous stew of mushrooms and giblets, and raspberry sherbet.

On Sunday when I awoke, Mr. D. had already left to go to the vineyard. Outside it wasn't as hot as it had been but there was a greater possibility of rain, and by this time I felt I couldn't bear it if it rained. A copy of the *Los Angeles Times* was in the kitchen and I looked through the weekly Calendar section, where all the local cultural events are hashed over. If I were living in Bakersfield, I wondered, would I long to go to Los Angeles to see *Chinatown*? No, I thought. It's too far.

At dinner the night before, Frank and the others had decided to play baseball the next morning. Now, I can take a lot of Americanness and can even imagine enviously what it must be like to have your life ruled by seasons and the life spans of crops. But not baseball. I read somewhere once that baseball is the game of the Silent Majority.

"You don't want to play baseball?" I asked Frank, phrasing it like that. "I mean, not in this heat, do you?"

"Shall we go for a drive?" He thought quickly in spite of his apparent hangover. (Perhaps he didn't want to play baseball.)

A couple of hours later, Frank and I drove silently through a silent Sunday Bakersfield where nothing was alive but the churches. They were crammed with people dressed too warmly for the town.

We passed a whole field, acres of torn-out plum trees, torn out by their roots and lying on their dead sides still neatly in a row. ("He tore 'em out," Mr. D. told us later, "because he couldn't get anyone to pick 'em.")

"There's Kern Canyon," Frank said, pointing the dusty golden car east toward some distant hills that turned out to be the Sierras.

Kern County is shaped like Nebraska and encompasses parts of the western edge of the Mojave Desert and a bunch of the Sierras, then dips into the San Joaquin Valley and goes across to the eastern edge of the Coast Range.

The Kern River has chopped its way through solid rock to create a precarious canyon with a two-lane highway. The smell of the river and the trees that are knee-deep in water, the sight of children and their fathers fishing, the dangerous highway that reveals more elaborate river scenes each time you go around a curve, are wonderful changes after the flat immenseness of the valley.

The ascent into the mountains is so quick that suddenly it says "Sequoia National Park," while on the other side of these Sierras the great Mojave Desert stands waiting. Inside these mountains is Lake Isabella, a man-made lake surreally available for water skiers and speedboat racers. No trees are in sight.

We drove around the lake for a long time and finally got to Kernville, where a few trees started to stand, but it wasn't until we drove up, up, up to maybe four thousand feet, to Glennville, that it was truly The Mountains. Giant sequoias cast their green smell quickly through the car and it all happened so fast, these abrupt California changes of altitude and landscape. The old schoolteacher thing about how California had the lowest point in the United States, Death Valley, only eighty miles away from the highest, Mount Whitney, came traipsing in from ancient classrooms.

Glennville seemed to me like a cowboy mountain dream. There were cows where there weren't sequoias, and when we stopped in the only café/bar in town we were approached by a James Dean type, an adorable young man who told me, straight-faced, that he was a cowboy.

"Are the mountain lions still giving you trouble?" Frank asked.

"No, they're pretty well gone now," the cowboy said. "What we got now is bears. These bears come and kill the cattle. My pa and I finally had to go out and shoot one, he was eating so many of our calves..."

"Shoot one?" I asked.

"Yeah, we rode out into the mountains with rifles..."

"How'd you know where it was?" Frank asked.

"Dogs," he smiled. "We found him, too, and my pa shot him."

There is a rodeo in Glennville at the beginning of every June and our twenty-two-year-old James Dean friend rides bareback horses. He wore a cowboy hat with the eye of a peacock feather stuck in the band, and he was one of those creatures so young and almost mystically cheerful that he seemed doomed.

"Doesn't he know," I asked Frank, "that peacock feathers are fatal?"

On the Country Music Awards on TV the other night, when they started giving prizes for the best "group" they said, "A group consists of two people, which is a duet; three people, which is a crowd; four people, which is a mob; and five people, which is the town council of Bakersfield."

"Come on," Frank said, "I'll take you to The Blackboard."

Everywhere we'd gone there'd been country music playing in the background. The Blackboard, Frank told me, was a great place to go dancing to country music—unless the Hell's Angels were there, though he was pretty sure they'd been banished. (Bakersfield, after all, is where Merle Haggard lives; they call it Nashville West.)

"I haven't been there for a long time," Frank said. "I know it'll be great."

On the way, Frank told me that until that night he hadn't felt that he'd come home. He'd been in Bakersfield a month but because there was so much work to do at the ranch he'd seen no one and been nowhere. Now at last he was going to The Blackboard.

The Blackboard is a big ordinary room, not too organized, and you don't have to pay to get in or anything. There's a stage where a kind of charming-looking band plays country songs, there's a nice big dance floor, there are tables and chairs, and opposite from the stage running the whole length of the room is a bar. A cop at the door asked for my I.D.—a wonderful moment.

For the first time since I'd arrived in the town it looked like I might have a recklessly good time and I began ordering double tequilas, much to Frank's amazement since my sobriety of the night before had convinced him of my solid good sense. But the night before didn't seem like such fun. The Blackboard looked like it might twirl into heaven with just another double tequila.

When we first came in, only the jukebox was playing. But the band's breaks were short and soon they were playing again, Everly

Brothers songs and two disguised Chuck Berry numbers that sounded like country songs. Then came a sort of slow dance song, and that's when we saw him.

From out of the wings he came, an archetypal ex-marine with a Dorothea Lange country girl in his arms, swirling and dipping with such elegance that the room became electric with dance.

The other dancers did their usual clumsy fox-trots but this didn't interfere with him. He had the girl in his arms and they danced divinely, never bumping into anyone; somehow they were everywhere and they were just great.

"Oh god, I wish I could dance like that," I told Frank, knowing I could never dance like that. The girl had closed her eyes and simply slipped around the floor on her toes like Cyd Charisse.

"Why don't you ask him?" Frank said.

"No!" I said. "I'd fall down in front of everyone and besides..."

But I knew if I didn't dance with this man that it would be one of those missed chances that puncture your life.

"Well, that's right anyway," Frank said, "because if you asked him his girlfriend would get mad and besides he probably wouldn't like it. I'll ask him for you."

"You!" I said. "What do you mean?"

"I'll tell him that the girl I'm with wants to dance with him."

"*No!*" I said, but he was up and doing it before I could say anything else.

I ordered another double tequila rather quickly and was halfway through it when Mr. Mike Lake came to our table and said to Frank, "Is it all right if I ask your lady to dance?"

Men, I thought, are so wonderful.

He was such a good dancer that I didn't have to do anything but close my eyes and be taken away, down the stream through the forest and up to the Magic Ball. Around we went, perfect, perfect, perfect, and I didn't fall down or die. I just was swept away in an ex-marine's arms straight into the clouds.

I was dancing, dancing through the crowded room and absolutely unable to stop smiling. Women who dance with their eyes closed, smiling, are as near to heaven as you can get on earth, and there I was, in heaven, only in Bakersfield.

We wound up in an all-night coffee shop with Mike Lake and his brother and some others. They too knew the James Dean cowboy and called him "the kid" so that I thought again about the peacock feather he'd so innocently stuck into his hatband and thought I'd like to weep tequila tears for the inevitable extinction of certain American boys on horseback.

The next morning I awoke with a hangover lending distance to my senses, and feeling lost and tender.

Frank drove me back through the golden hills, the wild rye, into the tiny town of Arvin, where we stopped for coffee in the Circle Dot Café. I knew he'd be working all day in the shed, loading more grapes and having lunch served by the ladies in the little house. I'd be driving back to L.A. with a boxful of peaches for my friends at the restaurant, to brandy and make sophisticated.

We stood by my car and it was 8:00 a.m. "Be sure and thank your father for me," I said. "I had a wonderful time. And when you come to L.A. I'll take you around, but I can't imagine it'll be half as... great as this."

"It will," Frank said, positive that it would.

"But..." I said, "...well, anyway, thank you."

I drove back through the vineyards and got onto the highway called "The Grapevine" because it twists through the Tehachapis every which way. I followed a giant truck filled with tomatoes until we began to climb the hills that separated me from the rest of the country and from my strange fan who'd liked my piece about Hollywood because it reminded him, so far away in his shilling-heated room and rainy London days, because it reminded him of home.

# THE FLIMSIES

*I think it was around this guy that I began to wonder if anything was ever going to be nice again. He never understood anything I said. He always treated me with kindly animal gentleness, but when he started telling me that his friends thought that "At last he's found a girl intelligent enough for him," I thought, Intelligent! I was intelligent enough for* him? *Besides, he was too tall.*

WE WERE hurried along Broadway by one of those wicked winds from the bay that follow you everywhere in San Francisco. Up hills and down around corners, greeting you where you least expect them, cold. Tears were trying to slide down either cheek because of the wind and my contact lenses, but they couldn't—the wind diverted them. I made us stop for a moment so I could blow my nose and he was still talking, expounding on his great drunken theory with greatly drunken Irish stamina. He was saying: "And so the most important thing is work . . ."

"Uh-huh," I said, sponging the tears and wiping my nose.

"That really is the most important thing for people like us . . . For *any*body! But mainly for people like us. Even if we love each other, and you know I love you, the most important thing is to keep working."

I could see how he'd have to think that, Jesus Christ, if for one moment he actually stopped working, my god, his whole world would cave in simultaneously and he'd drink himself straight into the cold but windless ground.

"Are you O.K.?" he inquired parenthetically and with swoonable charm.

"Yep," I sniffle.

"Are you leaving before noon?"

I nod, sort of. He took my elbow, and once more into the wind, dear friends, and his voice is lifted and carried over the top of North Beach. He says, "So it's *work*! Of anything, that's the most important."

I listen because he is an original man and he's thought about how to live, drink, laugh, and flirt around, and apparently all these are possible if one works, constantly, throughout. But I must know this already since I have managed over the last few years to devise projects, self-invented momentum. Irons in the fire. This last spring, my thirty-second spring, I actually pulled myself into such a concentrated little handful that I fashioned three goals from thin air. And only one of them fell by the wayside, but I have a superstitious feeling I invented that one to throw to the wolves as I slid through the snow on my tinkling sled to Moscow, safe and sound. (It was the only goal that had nothing to do with work.)

We stopped under a lamp and he took my shoulders in his Irish hands and looked straight at me, smiling. "So you understand then about work?"

"Yep," I said.

"Good. Let's go get a drink. There's a bar right across over there…"

The night was young and the moon was silver and the Irish have never been boring.


L.A. was embarrassing; I tried not to notice. The PSA plane had taken off from San Francisco, where everything was shipshape blue and white, a place for everything and everything in its place, and where does it land? Sprawlsberg. Ninety degrees, smog all over everything, giant glum vistas. No wonder writers from the East so joyfully leap upon the old L.A. tradition with cries of "ugly! plastic! wasteland!" PSA had decided to improve upon its only saving grace by removing itself from the sublime old Fred MacMurray airport and building next to it a nice new slummish-looking structure with an interior color scheme of rabid mock pink, orange, and crimson. So now, when you land in Burbank, you don't get off in an indigenous Lockheed mild tile-green beauty of an airport that is in harmony with the surroundings; no. *Now* you get off and pow! you're smack in the middle of…L.A.! It's embarrassing if you love L.A.

I am overjoyed to see my VW sitting there expectantly. I throw my heavy polo coat into the back seat, my overnight bag next to me in front. My claustrophobia from San Francisco begins to vanish— that cheerful shipshape vitality of the north violates my spirit and I long for vast sprawls, smog, and luke nights: L.A. It is where I work best, where I can live, oblivious to physical reality.

The notes for the story assigned to me by the fancy Eastern magazine sing in my memory and I begin to think of my typewriter waiting at home.

Hollywood Way is the name of the street from the airport, to Warner Brothers, to Barham, and then onto Cahuenga where greenery and the Hollywood Bowl and the traffic are my own. My court looks like something in a colonial English outpost, subtropical. Not too insane, really. Each little bungalow has its own view of the inner court where a jacaranda tree, since it's July, is lavender petals against the sky. (In August all the flowers drop to the earth.) Nabokov said in an interview lately that if he moved to America he'd live in L.A. because of the jacarandas. All those lavender flowers, like cotton-candy clouds. A pepper tree is at the end of our court. An old lady who grew up in Hollywood told me that once all the streets here were lined with pepper trees and then the cars came and they died. This one, set back from the street and protected by our bungalows, endures.

Twilight comes and I find I'm still sprawled out on my bed looking out the window, and the phone rings. It's the Irish voice from the north, telephoning from a bar.

"What are you doing?" he asks.

"Nothing," I say. "I'm just sort of empty."

"Down?"

"Well . . . maybe . . ."

"Have you finished your piece?"

"Practically."

"Work on something else then. When you're down, you should always work."

He'd never understand about the weather, that outside it's turned pink and the jacaranda tree is magenta, and next door the fourteen-year-old Mexican girl has finished her paper route and swung her long California-bred legs off her bike and now throws a Frisbee at her brother's head, expertly.

"Yes," I say, "... maybe tomorrow I'll get started on something."

"Your voice sounds so ... different."

"It's O.K.," I tell him. "Don't worry."

"I miss you," he says, with ceremony. I know what bar he's in, I can hear them calling the bartender, one of the bars we were in the night before. But all that work is his secret, not mine. Mine is looking out the window.

"Come out to dinner," my actress-friend calls to say, "I don't have to work tomorrow."

This actress "works." She's one of the one percent in "this town" in the Screen Actors Guild who can support themselves. The other ninety-nine percent presumably live half-lives of expectation. Because she has always worked, she never refers to Hollywood as "this town." "This town" is a phrase to be spoken in tones of bitterness as proof of corruption (e.g., "The only way to get anywhere in 'this town' is to sell your ass"). The minute I hear those words spoken earnestly, I grow uneasy and bored. Occasionally I'll refer to Hollywood as "this town," but only if the other person understands about irony.

"What shall we drink?" she asked, when we sat down in the restaurant. We drank the same thing when we were together for some reason, maybe symmetry.

"Tequila!" I said. I drank tequila in San Francisco to warm me up and in L.A. because it was appropriate.


He was just huge, this guy. There he was, coming into the restaurant looking like ... sports. He walked like ... then I knew ... basketball. Toes pointed slightly in, leg muscles too intense for city streets, like a Ferrari. His smile was straight out of an 8 × 10 glossy and I decided what the hell. Dimples, too.

He drank beer with his friends and afterward he told me that *he* had picked *me* up. He was obviously an actor.

"An *actor*!" my actress friend Charlotte whoops. "You!? I thought you knew better."

"I do," I answer. "But this one's . . . so *big*!"

"But darling," she insists, "let me just say this one thing. With actors, first they find out what you like, and then they do it. They instinctively understand. But it's not real. You know?"

"Well, it'll be something to see what I like," I said. "I've forgotten." (I mean if someone's going to know instinctively what you want, you may as well find out what it is.)

For three days I am smothered in luxury. Nothing is too trivial or too much to ask. Burritos and champagne. I don't even have to go outdoors in the smog. On the fourth evening, my sister drops by.

My sister is small, light, beautiful, with no hips and perfect breasts. I am fifteen pounds overweight, which I can forget sometimes until my sister appears. I am sort of invincible looking and I never display any of those womanly qualities so praised through the ages, like modesty, tact, or sweet vulnerability. My sister, on the other hand, always looks as though her favorite kitten just got run over.

"Your sister is very beautiful," he says when she leaves.

"Oh yeah?" I harden. "Well, look, if you'd prefer my sister, please don't think you have to hang around here because she and I have gone through enough of that shit to last forever!" (You can see, can't you, how my generous spirit and diplomatic nature just rise to these occasions.) And I add for one last observation, "Men are all creeps!"

He looked surprised. Then he took my hand in his giant paw and said in low, slightly astonished tones, "I would *never* interfere in anything as delicate as the relationship between you and your sister."

When I told this story later, every woman I met gasped, strangled in disbelief. "No, *really*!" they said. "A *man* said that? I don't believe it."

Only Charlotte said, "See! What'd I tell ya?"

"What?"

"About actors! They find out what you like and then they . . ."

"I can't believe that," I said. "He's simply not smart enough."

"It's not smarts," she insisted. "It's gut instinct. That's how actors work. Brains don't matter one bit. Some of the best actors on earth are complete idiots."

But "delicate," I thought to myself, turning it around and around in my mind like a dream of jacarandas.

And perhaps the dream could have gone on unbroken, except that they never do. One of the reasons was that he snuck a look at the flimsies and found out he was either going to die or turn into a vegetable.

He'd been playing Andrew Broston, an architect cuckold, on this soap opera for five years. Although the plots of soap operas are closely guarded secrets so that no leakage will flow out into the audience, there is an outline of the future of the soap opera written sketchily, in pages known as The Flimsies—the plot, without actual scenes, is basically followed from this flimsy line of the story. So one day my basketball player/actor saw the flimsies unattended and he found out that the plane Andrew Broston was taking to New York to accuse his wife of infidelity was going to make a crash landing. He would be badly hurt but linger on, it said in the flimsies, and "never be able to speak again, remaining a human vegetable."

"*I* am not going to turn into a vegetable," he declared, and I thought, in a moment of uncharacteristic compassion, that I'd make the poor thing dinner.

I don't really know if it was the flimsies or the dinner but I've often noticed that there is a moment when a man develops enough confidence and ease in a relationship to bore you to death. Sometimes one hardly even notices it's happened, that moment, until some careless remark arouses one's suspicions. I have found that what usually brings this lethargy on is if the woman displays some special kindness. Like making dinner.

After that dinner he could hardly keep his eyes open. His conversation, which had once been wonderfully peppered with words like "delicate," folded in the days that followed into a continuous barrage against his agent, the producer of the soap, the writers, and "this town." Now I didn't raise myself to be the charming woman I am today in order to listen to some actor talk about "this town." (I'd forgotten how awful it could be.)

Finally, one night, we were on our way downtown on the freeway to the post office, where he was making a last sad pilgrimage to mail replies to his poor fans who, three weeks behind, didn't realize he was going to get on a plane that would crash and turn him into a vegetable. (He had fans everywhere; people were always coming up to him on the street and commiserating with him about his horrible wife cuckolding him.)

"I can't stand it anymore," I said. "I hate hearing about agents."

"Oh yeah?" he snapped. "Well maybe you hate me too."

Oh god, I said to myself. I shouldn't have said anything. I just should have shut up and gone home and hoped he'd die on the soap and get better in real life. I never should have made him dinner.

The reflection from the 7:00 p.m. sunset turned the eastern sky lavender, the clouds behind us burnt orange. But I was too numbed to like it, and his body that had been so taut was now grimly earthbound.

The thing is, I *know* you can't make them dinner. Not a mouthful, not if they're dying. In Japan, I understand, it's considered obscene to eat in the same room as someone of the opposite sex.

"I'm coming down there tomorrow," the Irish San Franciscan telephoned to say. "Let's have drinks."

We went to the Polo Lounge (although it was not his lowdown kind of place at all). It was 3:00 p.m. and the serious movie people had returned to the hills after their business lunches. The Irishman and I ordered gorgeous Bloody Marys and he took my hand and looked into my eyes, smiling. It had been only six weeks since I'd seen him. He was wonderful.

"What have you been doing?" he said.

"Oh . . . You know . . ." I said. I couldn't say basketball.

"Have you been working?"

"Well, I . . ."

"What about your book?" he asked. "Have you talked to your agent yet about what you're going to do?"

"I was going to, only I've been . . . Let's not talk about agents," I suggest.

The waiter brings him more vodka "to dilute the boring taste of the tomato juice," as he puts it. He lifts his glass to me and says, "You're looking wonderful."

The cats, the ones who sleep on the roof around the patio of the Polo Lounge, have begun stretching on the eaves and one or two are now climbing down the branches of the tree in the patio. All the cats at the Beverly Hills Hotel are tabbies.

"You know," he says, kissing the inside of my palm, "I missed you."

He is dressed in tweeds and tailoring whereas I look as though I've been roused from a bed of bonbons, ostrich feathers, and tuxedo highballs. I watch him observe, with the merest flicker of disapproval, two young men, actors probably, who await the maître d' at the entrance and are still wearing their damp white tennis clothes. They are impatient and slightly barbaric, their legs are tight as springs. Ahhhh, me.

I shift my eyes to the window again and outside to the patio where an orange-and-brown striped kitty has just leapt from a branch to the ground.

I wonder if . . . (one of the tennis actors slides me a look) . . . I wonder if I'll ever be able to have what I like or if my tastes are too various to be sustained by one of anything. I wonder if I'll ever be able to get my big huge basketball player back like he was before. Or are all my occasional romances to fall to the ground after a month or so, like the jacaranda flowers? I always seem to end up with these Irishmen, drinking strong spirits, having to resist actors who know what I like, however delicate and flimsy it may be.

# DODGER STADIUM

*You won't like this piece because you don't like baseball so you can just skip it. Besides, this man means nothing to me. Hardly.*

THE WAY to make it rain is to wash your car, as everyone knows (you can make it drizzle if you do only your windshields, but rain requires a whole car), and the way to get invited to a fancy French restaurant is to have rustled yourself up a nice, cozy omelette so that just as everyone has decided to go out for dinner and calls you, you're sitting there in your pajamas, thinking how virtuous you are for being home. So, if you want to get invited to something not quite dinner, you could make scrambled eggs with no bread on the side but melted cheese in the scrambled eggs or something, to show God that you are serious about staying home and being virtuous. His interest is then piqued as He seeks to devise an appropriate temptation for you to succumb to.

I had just finished making myself some nice scrambled eggs in my brand-new Teflon pan with not only cheese but this newfangled great *whipped* chive cream cheese, and it was Saturday and only 5:30. (I had considered putting chorizo, that Mexican sausage, in, but chorizo has so much garlic in it that if you make anything out of *that* someone you barely know who's wildly attractive will turn up and I just wasn't up to one of those, Saturday night or no.)

I settled down before the television to a *Saratoga Trunk* rerun and had finished my last delicious fluffy bite (that cream cheese is so fluffy) when the phone rang.

"Listen," he said—he never had to say his name, our voices were imprinted on each other's aural hearts—"I've been in this damn town of yours for a week now and I've been locked in the studio from six in the morning until eleven at night and I've *got* to get out of here. The Dodgers are playing the Giants and I thought you might..."

"Baseball..." I correctly assumed. I had this immediate feeling that he was about to tell me he was going with some friends and that if he could get out of it later, he'd take me to dinner.

"Well, I know it isn't the type of thing you usually do, but..."

"You want *me* to go with you?"

"Yeah, well, I thought maybe we'd just...But if you'll be bored..."

"Baseball? *Me?*" I said, attributing the whole thing to the cream cheese. It *had* to be the cream cheese.

"But I'd love to," I said. "When do we..."

"I'll pick you up in fifteen minutes. Dress warm."

I've been halfway around the world in a plane and witnessed revolutions in Trafalgar Square, but nobody has ever asked me to see a baseball game in my whole American life. People take me to screenings of obscure films, they drag me along to fashionable new nightclubs, they have me meet them in a taxi, honey, and whisk me off to dangerous Cuban samba places to *bailar* the night away. They don't take me to baseball games—it wouldn't occur to them. No wonder I'm such a sitting duck for this man. He is the only one who could take me out to a ball game, but then *he* could take me to a flower show in Pomona, and it wouldn't be any stranger than the idea of us together is already.

I remember the first time I saw him. It was at a reception for a nouveau-wave actress in a bungalow behind the Beverly Hills Hotel, and everyone was making faded, jaded little French remarks at each other and being tiresome because the toast for the caviar wasn't buttered enough—when in he came, dressed like Johnny Carson and asking for Scotch.

I pounced on him and lured him off to the sidelines.

"Do you think these shoes are too purple?" I asked.

"Too purple?" he said, looking down at my feet. "If they're not *too* purple, they're not purple *enough*."

And there, on that cold marble floor in that tricky company, I fell hopelessly in love without a backward glance and wondered what a nice girl like me was doing in a place like that.

In this day and age of men and women ducking for cover until whatever results from radical feminism and the general gory corruption riddling the country from stem to stern, I fell right smack in love with an obvious American man. In my mind, from that moment forward, I always thought of him as The Last American. It was too bad Henry James couldn't have seen him, the way he wore his store-bought clothes with such lithe nonchalance that he put to shame the other men in the room with their narrow Parisian shirts and Milanese tailors. He was obviously too busy to think beyond a turtleneck and an all-right jacket, but he was so artlessly physical that he was Astaire himself. Very American.

He was even too busy for the outcome of the game between men and women. He probably hadn't even noticed it. And I understood everything perfectly after that: Men and women are stuck with each other. Men go to parties they don't really like because women want to go, and women in love go to baseball games and are graceful about it, though they never would have thought it up all by themselves. It's very relaxing being stuck.

And so there he was, fifteen minutes later, an impatient, suspicious man brought up in a tradition of being kept waiting by women.

"I'm ready," I said, and was.

"You going to be warm enough?"

"Fur coat," I answered, throwing it over my arm and following him out the door into a sunlit late afternoon. Once we were safely driving (after he opened the car door for me—he's from another era, too, not just the opposite sex), I asked, "Tell me about baseball, about you and baseball..."

"Oh...it's very boring," he said, maybe having doubts.

We took Sunset because the night before fifty thousand people had jammed the freeway around the stadium. His logistics were always elegant—a personality trait that saved the studio untold millions every year.

"It isn't even a very important game," he said. "It's only the eleventh of the season..."

"So it doesn't matter?" I wondered.

"Well, if you win the first one and the second and keep on," he explained, "it adds up." The way he drove a car was the most inexplicable thing about him; he drove with an absent-minded, almost puttering kindliness, as though when he was inside a car, the world got slower; it was time for reverie almost. "You know," he said dreamily, "I haven't been to a game in ... five years. When I was a kid, I was a fanatic. We used to go out and watch 'em practice."

"Who?"

"The Dodgers," he said, as though there was no other team.

"Well, can't you watch on television?"

"The phone isn't going to stop ringing just because I'm watching TV," he said.

"Well, aren't you glad you don't have one of those little bleepers in your pocket like doctors?" I looked on the bright side.

"Oh Jesus," he cringed.

We arrived at the wide tollgate-looking parking lot by about 6:15 and into the vast circular maze of parkdom which was already more than half filled, and he nudged the car into a lot that sort of looked like it was the one under a sign that said anyone without a green sticker would be towed away, and there he parked. I had never seen him do anything reckless before.

"What if they tow the car away?" I hated to be a wet blanket, but, still...

"It's rented," he pointed out. "And, besides, it's no good and I was going to take it back in the morning and get another one."

"Well...O.K." I could just see us way up there with no car, tramping down to Sunset and trying to get a cab. I decided not to worry about it.

We walked upward toward the stadium with all those people. At first I hadn't noticed anything because the people looked like the hordes who frequented every gigantic event I ever went to. They were young, in their twenties, and they wore jeans and pea coats and they all had long hair (later, looking down from our seats at all that hair brought it home to me how much those shampoo companies must take in). The only difference was that there were a lot of little kids—a *lot* of little kids. The kids all had long hair, too. Wait a minute, I thought to myself, I thought baseball was ... I mean, I thought people who went to places I never went, like baseball games, were all fat, middle-aged, blue-collar workers holding Pabst Blue Ribbon. Or, at the very least, the well-scrubbed Young Republicans with their crew cuts and their girlfriends with freckles. All *these* people looked like they were going to a Dylan concert.

"Look at these people," I gushed. "I thought everyone here would be..."

"*My* age, right?" He gave me a very calculated, cold look. Oh god, I thought, *now* what have I done?

"No, older," I tried to patch up. For the first time in my life I did not envy his wife in New York; penthouse, fur coats, anything. He had never been angry with me before, but now I saw he could be; it was scary.

But then the feeling of baseball coming closer did something to him, and he shrugged and put his arm around me. A close one.

We got our tickets and strolled inside the gates where music was playing and hawkers were hawking, and he bought himself a scorecard and became downright cheerful. The blissfully festive smell of mustard cut through the air dissolving any residual anger, and zillions of little kids with pennants and blue plastic Dodger caps raced through the young couples as we all gave ourselves up to the setting sun. The tempo of the organ music inflicted the reality so that everything belonged inside of these Vatican Stadium walls, and the studios, and phones, and death, and rented cars belonged outside if they wanted any claims on time or space.

I love hordes. They screen out free choice; you're free at last: stuck.

Our seats were way up. They were around third base so we could see over the tops of the bleachers on the other side and out to the green hills in the coming twilight beyond. The green hills had violent purple ice plants on them and looked like a scratch in the world bleeding purple blood. The baseball field below was gorgeous. It was the first I'd ever seen, but I'm sure other people must think it's a beautiful one. The grass all mowed in patterns like Japanese sand gardens and the dirt all sculpted in swirling bas-relief.

"It's so beautiful," I gushed.

"Not bad," he agreed.

All the people were beginning to fill up the seats around us and the whole event just took over; it became completely itself, in a kind of very loose tension like inside a love affair. You can care or not care at a baseball game, just so long as you're inside the gates. You can casually chat with your friend and know that if anything happens you won't miss it for the crowd will alert you and carry you through.

At seven o'clock, this terrible lady sang a moribund version of "The Star-Spangled Banner" as we stood, and I saw one man, the only one there who looked like a blue-collar cartoon, remove his cap for the occasion. Otherwise, it was all long hair or blue plastic souvenir caps on little kids. Then we all sat down and waited.

Baseball is easy to fathom, not like football, which people explain to me at great length and I understand for one brief moment before it all falls apart in my brain and looks like an ominous calculus problem. The tension in baseball comes in spurts between long waits where everyone can forget about it, a perfectly lifelike rhythm.

"That's your team," he explained when we first sat down and guys were out in the huge field aimlessly warming up. "The home team always wears white and the other gray."

"*My* team?" I almost scoffed. I mean, I'll go along with him to a baseball game gracefully, but he didn't expect me to take sides, did he? But it was too late because somehow, before the thing even started, I had acquired an intense, fierce loyalty to the Dodgers, and I don't know how it happened. I never expected that my external personality, which had hardened into that of a blasé Hollywood lady of fashion, could rupture at the first sight of those Americans down there in their white uniforms, but there it was. I was hooked. Early in life I discovered that the way to approach anything was to be introduced by the right person. Like the first time I smelled caviar, I put it right back down on the plate and waited five years until a Russian countess offered it to me again with cold vodka in her exile's parlor and *then* I loved it. (I didn't want to be one of those people who don't like caviar.) I had always thought, however, that baseball was never going to happen to me, but I hadn't counted on The Last American making me a Dodgers fan, all of a sudden.

The game started just as night began to fall, and he tried to explain to me what was happening and would happen and why forty-seven thousand people grumbled and moaned one moment and forty-seven thousand people cheered or yelled "charge" the next. A great deadpan man climbed up and down the aisles catching quarters brilliantly and throwing ice-cream sandwiches back with amazing grace, while below us incredibly agile men caught high flies with similar but grander perfection.

"Watch how fast that guy throws," he told me about the pitcher, and I watched as this ball slammed through the air much too seriously for it to be only a game. The pitcher, I decided, was a strangely serious person in all of this hurry-up–wait to-do.

Over the top of the opposite grandstand was one lone palm tree trying to sneak in. That palm tree was all that existed of Los Angeles, or anything, outside—the only way you could tell you were even in Southern California and not just in baseballdom. He told me that the last game he'd been to had been arranged by the studio and that they'd sat in the loges behind home plate, the best seats. But, unlike Dylan concerts, it doesn't really matter where you're sitting in baseball, or even if you sit at all, because some of the little kids never sat—they barreled up and down the aisles totally absorbed in any action at all that should fall their way. And it doesn't matter if you yawn; yawning is a luxury that befits all that tension.

"No wonder everyone loves this," I told him. "It's so . . ."

"Awww, come on," he smiled disparagingly, "you don't really . . ."

But just then this damn Giant hit a home run! The forty-seven thousand people were riveted to that ball, the outfielder was running backward, and he almost . . . almost . . . But he didn't.

"Ohhhhhhh," we all remarked.

"How could those damn Giants *do* that!" I groaned. "They're not going to *win* are they?"

I was clutching his arm rather tightly.

"Calm down," he said.

"But they *can't* win!"

It had been a comfortable three-to-one in our favor, and now it was three-to-two! And now that it *was* three-to-two, the whole place came alive with worry. No casual chitchat now, by gum, I thought with my elbows on my knees and my thumbnail in my teeth. By the ninth inning it was still three-to-two and the damn Giants came up to bat throwing in cheating pinch hitters and anything else they had up their sleeves. If they got even one point the thing would be tied and it would go into extra innings (and it was getting cold). They had two men on base; the Dodgers had a pitcher who was very makeshift, since the other pitcher had collapsed in front of everyone after throwing just one ball. Most of the Dodgers, in fact, I learned were in the hospital trying to get well, and in the game I saw, two more fell apart. So this novice was pitching, and the damn Giants had two men on base and all they had to do was hit a home run and all would be lost. But, just as I was succumbing to glumness, a wonderful third baseman caught a third out, effortlessly, and so not only didn't we have to stay for extra innings, we also got out early and *won* to boot!

"We won! We won! We *won*!" I cried gleefully.

"Did you really like that?" he asked, finally believing me.

"Yeah. What'll we go to next?"

"Hockey, when they're playing..." he thoughtfully decided.

"Oh, goody," I said. We had joined the hordes in the exodus to the parking lot and the ensuing chaos of trying to get out of that otherwise well-designed place. We got stuck in the parking scene forever (twenty minutes), and he fell into another reverie.

"You know," he began, "when I was a kid, I tried out for the Dodgers."

"You did?" I tried to imagine him in white and could, perfectly. "You'd have been great, I think," I said.

"I made it all the way to the finals," he continued. "I was only seventeen. I might have made it in the next season, only the war..." (He meant World War II, when he was a lieutenant or something in the Army, and my parents were married to other people and hadn't even considered having me.)

"What part did you try out for?" I asked quickly, remembering that cold, calculating anger, which was to be avoided at all costs.

"Pitcher," he said.

"And so what happens when you're the pitcher?"

"Well... You have a pretty good life. You work six months a year, you practice a couple of months, and then you're off."

"It sounds kind of like your life now," I offered.

But he wasn't listening, and he went on, "And if you behave yourself and don't get into a lot of trouble, you wind up coaching a team or managing..." His wistful voice faded out and then returned to a more realistic tone. "Awww, but I probably wouldn't have been good enough."

"You know what I wish?" I said; the traffic had at last untangled and we were beginning to move. "I wish I had one of your double Scotches."

"You know what?" he said. "So do I. Where shall we go?"

"Well, luckily we still have the car," I said, "so we can go anywhere."

Later, as we sat in this hidden little French restaurant, having gotten our Scotch and ordered, I looked at him and thought he would have made a great pitcher, but if he had, I never would have met him; he never would have found himself in his Hollywood/ New York life of studios and girls in bungalow receptions who take one look and find him exotically American enough to pounce on.

He turned his glass in his hands easily, innocent of the motions of a startled agent at the next table who leapt to his feet and was upon us, plunging us into the great Hollywood pastime: movie-deal talk.

"Jesus, I been tryin' to get ahold of you for two weeks..." the agent began, sliding down into our booth.

The anonymous freedom of the hordes had so stuck in The Last American's eyes that he blinked twice at this otherwise familiar face, trying to remember where they'd met, but it didn't take him long to recall what the deal was, only a few seconds for his strange boyish eyes to rise to the occasion. He laughed, patted the agent on the shoulder, and quickly managed to shrug off his amnesia.

I felt myself fading into the background and let their voices wash over me, well aware of my place in this traditional back-street romance. There was plenty of time to worry about who was taking advantage of whom in the war between men and women or the future of the country or any of that. I felt The Last American's hand reach under the table and come to rest someplace just above my knee, and I suddenly thought how fortunate it was that I hadn't had my car washed that afternoon.

# HEROINE

*You'll probably think I'm being too extravagant with Terry, that I've attributed things to her that do not exist. (Especially after the night she said "fuck you" to a cop in Beverly Hills and very nearly got us all busted.) But counterbalancing all this is her performance. And she's promised not to drink anymore in front of strangers, promised. Anyway, she helped me in a strange sort of a way when I was really down, down, down. And we have to stick together or else heroine-ism will find us home alone with no women to go out drinking with, and in America this can lead to stronger spirits, wilder music, and an early grave.*

OUT IN Santa Monica there is a huge building with many floors and lots of its own beach front. It appears so festive on hot days when the sea breezes blow the canvas awnings hither and yon, that you might like to live there. In order to do so, you must first convince some tough observers that you are fit, and second, you must turn over all your worldly goods like your car, money, and furniture. Then you will be allowed to enter Synanon. I knew one woman who convinced them that she was a junkie (she was a fine actress), but actually she'd never injected heroin. Three months later in one of those marathon games, she confessed her non-addiction. They were so mad, they made her shave her head.

"How come you wanted to go there in the first place?" I asked her. Now she lives in the valley, is married, and takes courses at night school. "I mean you had to give them your car for god's sakes."

"I've always liked the beach," she told me. "And I never had a father."

"Oh," I said.

"It was fine there until the director decided that since he was going to stop smoking cigarettes, we all had to stop."

Having quit smoking, I knew what she meant. Unless one is in the exact right mood, it's impossible. Smoking has been so glamorous for so long, all those matches, those pauses, the lipstick on the tips—the smoke itself curling its casual way through the most nerve-wracking moments. But in another way, smoking, although glamorous, has never been as glamorous as heroin—and dying from cigarettes just doesn't have the tragic sunset quality that O.D.ing lends to death. Heroin is the celebrated romantic excess of our time.

It's been a long time since I thought seriously about heroin, but yesterday, having drinks with Terry Finch, I remembered everything I'd ever felt with total recall.

I heard that when someone once asked William Burroughs why he took heroin he explained simply, "So I can get up and shave in the morning."

Another memory was the time I was going to try to convince Janis Joplin to let me do her album cover. A mutual friend was to introduce us. We went to the recording studio and entered the producer's panelboard room and the *sound* was so loud that my whole body recoiled in pain. The producer had become so deaf that it had to be that loud for him to hear it. Janis Joplin was asleep on the floor.

"How can she be asleep?" I shouted.

"What?" the producer asked.

Two days later the mutual friend tried again and this time we went to the Landmark Motor Hotel. It was daytime. We entered the courtyard swimming area and there, in the pool, with a grayish-white Irish washerwoman complexion and wearing a black one-piece bathing suit, was Janis Joplin, floating. The blue pool flickered around her.

"Is she dead?" I mumbled. I was afraid.

"We'll come back," my friend said as we backed out.

A week later she died. And people wondered how she could do such a dumb thing to herself when she had everything.

Women are prepared to suffer for love; it's written into their birth certificates. Women are not prepared to have "everything," not success-type "everything." I mean, not when the "everything" isn't about living happily ever after with the prince (where even if it falls through and the prince runs away with the baby-sitter, there's at least a *precedent*). There's no precedent for women getting their own "everything" and learning that it's not the answer. Especially when you got fame, money, and love by belting out how sad and lonely and beaten you were. Which is only a darker version of the Hollywood "everything" in which the more vulnerability and ineptness you project onto the screen, the more fame, money, and love they load you with. They'll only give you "everything" if you appear to be totally confused. Which leaves you with very few friends.

The kinds of friends you get when you have "everything" (after your old friends have decided to send you all their screenplays, so that you're afraid to run into them lest they wonder why you haven't read them) are either your immediate family or other famous people. A lot of times your immediate family is what drove you into such excess in the first place. So that leaves other people with "everything." In Hollywood, there's usually a special grace period when you're allowed to grab a few friends before you're pitched into only meeting other famous people. The trick is to find friends who are sophisticated enough to understand what you're talking about but disinterested enough not to come to you with their screenplays. Sometimes it all happens so fast that there's no time to find real friends or else it happens and during the time you should be finding real friends you are still acting like you were before, waiting for the prince. So that when "everything" comes, one has nothing. Especially if you're a woman and waiting for a prince. Janis Joplin was always wondering when her prince would come, and the wait was such a bore that she purchased total surcease on the smooth, blank, clear, smiling lake of heroin. A famous friend of the famous.

The one time I came close to taking it myself was during a shaky week-long period of my life when I was confronted with the possibility that a book I'd written might become a best-seller. A curious pain curled up in my chest and neither Valium nor Wild Turkey seemed to be able to numb it. My old friends called on the phone and sounded different: "How did you get *that* stuff published?" they'd wonder baldly and add, "Well, now that you're a star, how does it feel?"

Trapped. There was no place to go but up. I had another drink.

"Why don't I come over with some heroin," this odd old friend of mine suggested. And he did drop by but I'd gone out. "Chicken," he sneered, "I knew you'd chicken out." (He had telephoned to sneer.)

Two days later he purchased some especially perfect junk and was killed. Nobody noticed for four days and then finally the police noticed the smell and removed him from the alley off Santa Monica Blvd.

(When someone dies of heroin, like magic two or three close friends spring up in his place to pay God back by becoming junkies themselves. Perversity is a correlate in all of this.)

I did not become famous but I got near enough to smell the stench of success. It smelt like burnt cloth and rancid gardenias, and I realized that the truly awful thing about success is that it's held up all those years as the thing that would make everything all right. And the only thing that makes things even slightly bearable is a friend who knows what you're talking about.

I first met Terry Finch when she had just signed with a record company that I was working for. The publicist whom I assisted was stunned with joy when it turned out that Terry Finch was not a monosyllabic, far-out, Topanga hippie. Although she was only twenty-six, she was completely in charge of herself. She even wrote her own bio, which turned out to be a long, beautiful poem about her hometown in North Dakota, her years in Rome, where she studied architecture, and her love for Hughe's Market. She was a star, I plainly saw.

It seems to me that you can have any sort of features to be a star, really, just so long as your skin is luminous. Most movie stars have that kind of skin up close. I don't know if they get it after they have become stars and people massage it into them, or if they become stars *because* they have it. Those who have it glow in the dark. The men, too, like Dean Martin and Tony Curtis. Mick Jagger used to look like a Gainsborough, but not lately. Maybe they're born with it.

Terry's skin was like that. Her features were interesting enough but would have passed unnoticed had it not been for her skin and her tawny, thick, billowing hair. Her eyes were a strange gray color, her teeth were small and white, and her inside bones were brittle lace. But she was covered with skin that always seemed as though she'd just stepped off the yacht, tan and poreless, with cheeks the color of baby's feet. One by one her eyelashes spiked their way around her gray eyes, a miracle of textures. Most people are either silver or gold but Terry was both, with her gray eyes in the midst of all that color. There she was, an ordinary slender girl with small breasts and no hips who could just make everything stop by entering a room. But she didn't want to; she wanted to sing.

She sang in a loud, unexpectedly raucous voice about losing her lover to the farm girl back home in North Dakota. She sat at the piano and hit her foot on the loud pedal as her birdlike hands slammed competently on those keys, her voice pealing out like Niagara Falls.

She really was a sight. I thought she was terrific. I played her records all the time and waited confidently for her to become a star, only nothing happened except the record company I worked for and she recorded for, folded.

I saw Terry a couple of times over the next years and in spite of what had not happened, I still was sure that such guileless vulnerability could not fade away unnoticed. Or would she, I began to wonder, become one of those strange eccentric women, too crazy to pass in society?

Once I met her at a party; she was wearing English riding pants, high boots, a cream silk blouse, and a narrow green corduroy jacket. Somehow it all combined to make her look like Errol Flynn as Robin Hood. We said hello and exchanged phone numbers.

When my book came out, Terry Finch telephoned and sounded pleased and not like the others asking how it felt to be "a star." She liked my book, she said, and had actually bought a copy and read it. There was a trace of wariness however when she asked if I ever had any free time to go out for a drink, and I told her my whole life was free time and why didn't we go right then. It was she, come to think of it, with whom I sat drinking when my odd friend with the heroin had dropped by and decided I was a chicken.

Terry and I had gone to the Formosa Café, which was down the street from my apartment. It's an old railroad car papered with 8 × 10 glossies of Betty Grable and Zachary Scott. We had rumaki and mai-tais.

"You know," she said, "I'm so happy about your book. It came out just when I had decided that I probably was never going to amount to anything and that I might as well go back to North Dakota, being out of bread with nothing happening. I thought your book was a good omen. And that night I met this director and he's giving me a part in this film he's doing."

"Oh, how wonderful," I said. It *was* wonderful, we could talk about something other than my being a trapped star. "When do they start shooting?"

"In the summer, in Spain. I'll get to see Spain all expenses paid and five thousand dollars." She picked up a rumaki by the toothpick and added, "And they're going to let me sing one of my songs in a nightclub scene."

We sat in the boxcar of the Formosa Café and dawdled away the afternoon, wondering about Spain.

I don't know how many months went by before I began to hear strange reports from far and wide that went: "Terry Finch is absolutely fantastic. She has stolen the movie away from everyone."

People who'd seen rushes at dailies and during editing came away shaken. People were jealous of me because I knew her.

The movie came out.

She appeared on the covers of *Vogue*, *Time*, and the Calendar section of the *L.A. Times*. *Esquire*, *Rolling Stone*, *The Village Voice*, and *Cosmopolitan* proclaimed her brilliant and gorgeous. She and the male lead went on a publicity blitz around America and were on every single talk show imaginable and no one gave her anything but love, even Johnny Carson, and you know how he is. In the movie she was fragile and dying of consumption; a vision of vulnerable loveliness cannot go unrewarded. So everyone just loved her. And I wondered, vaguely, what was going to happen when she sat down at the piano and belted out the one about the farm girl.

She returned to Los Angeles and I caught glimpses of her sitting in splendid company in restaurants and at parties, her hair tied back severely in a black ribbon. She became elegant; she was no longer Robin Hood. I saw her once in a blue cotton dress that came down to her feet and made her look like she was floating. And another time I saw her all in black with a black hat, looking like Garbo.

It was very difficult not to believe that she must now have "everything" in spite of my own recent brush with the truth. If I had met her after seeing that movie, I would have been angry if she played anything but lullabies on the piano, so intense was her glow in the dark. When she wasn't on the screen, all you could do was wait for her to return. And her song became an international hit single.

One night I ran into her at a party where we exchanged unlisted phone numbers and she said she'd call. Now that she was a star, I doubted she would.

"Listen," she said, two days later, "why don't you come over. I've got this Scotch."

Now that she was famous, I figured, we had to go to her house and not the Formosa but it seemed not too grandiose considering what had happened to her.

"I'd meet you somewhere," she explained, "but my car is fucked."

"Are you getting it fixed?" I asked.

"Fixed! It costs money to get that car fixed. Aha, you think I'm rich! I am *not* rich. I have no money. Hardly."

"Oh..." I said.

"*And*," she continued, "they've got warrants out so if I drive my car and get stopped they take me to jail."

"Oh..." I said.

"*And* I lost all my clothes in Cleveland."

"Didn't you make any money on the record?" I asked.

"They own it," she said. "But I do have this half a bottle of Scotch. So why don't you come on over."

After returning from the publicity tour, Terry had had to move out of her little bungalow that she'd lived in for five years because her phone number and address had been listed and she was now a star. It was not safe. She moved a few blocks away to an old Hollywood residential hotel, five flights up, overlooking Hollywood Blvd. From her windows, looking east, there was Hollywood Blvd. West was just plain Hollywood. And the mountain at the southern end of Laurel Canyon.

Her apartment was a disorderly mixture of ongoing projects. All the surfaces were piled high with music paper and piano scores, watercolors, amps, silk blouses, and cute shoes. Photographs and newspaper clippings were everywhere. Disorder had the upper hand.

We drank Scotch and tried to talk but the phone rang into every thought. Managers, lawyers, puzzling old acquaintances, on and on and on. She didn't sound glad to hear from anyone but her sister in North Dakota.

Terry had just returned from Sausalito, where she'd been making an album. She'd had to spend an extra week there because she hated the mix the producer had lazily produced and so she had to mix it herself.

"Do you know how to do that?" I wondered. When you make a record, all the different instruments play separately on separate tapes called tracks. At the end these tracks are mixed so that the bass guitar isn't too loud and the vocals are clear. This is done on a horrible panel with dials, buttons, knobs, and red lights. I just couldn't imagine Terry mixing. "How did you learn how to mix?"

"I learned because I *had* to," she said, grimly. "This whole damn album has been like pulling teeth. Every time I try and get them to do something, I have to throw a fit to have it be right. They were even going to pick my songs!"

After the fourth phone conversation with one manager, Terry got up, went across the shambled living room, took a cushion off the couch and socked it repeatedly. "All I meet now are businessmen with hair in their noses," she shouted, bellowed, "when all I want are nice young men with good manners!"

"Who doesn't?" I asked. "I know three right off the bat who are dying to meet you."

"You do?" She stopped socking the cushion.

"Yeah, and I'm having a party on Thursday; they'll all be there."

"Oh. I can't go. They're taking me to Cannes."

"Maybe . . ." I suggested, "you can find something there."

"In the daytime I do interviews and at night we go to screenings," she explained. "And there are no handsome young men with good manners in either place."

"They ought to fix women up the same way they do men out of town," I said. "It's not fair."

"Awww, but that's not how I want to do it. I don't want . . . I want, you know, *romance*. Mystery. You know who's been calling me?"

She told me the names of several famous rich handsome devils who're supposed to be the hottest bachelor catches around.

"Well," I said, "what's wrong with that?" She did have everything.

"I'm just new meat, fresh on the market. Anyway, if I'd wanted rich-boy folderol I could have stayed home in North Dakota. The guy I left to come here had forty million dollars. And he was nice. And cute too. But what I want now is a nice young man with good manners . . ." she paused to consider, "who gives great head."

"Let's go to Musso's and have Bloody Marys," I suggested.

"Oh!" She brightened. "Yes. Let's."

The Bloody Marys at Musso & Frank's Restaurant are unparalleled in Western thought and can cure anything. The festive limes and newly ground pepper along with the tomato juice all combine to smell like cinnamon.

Terry had had to curl her hair before we went because now she couldn't just go out, but within the hour we were ensconced in a cool, calm booth of red leather and solid wooden partitions glowing away in their own patina. People around us seemed to move in slow motion, the way extras do in movies when they want to give the illusion of a background of people without distracting you from the stars. We ordered sinless breakfasts: scrambled eggs and creamed spinach. (I don't care what time it is, I *always* get creamed spinach at Musso's. It's the nutmeg.)

"Mmmm," we said in unison, taking the first sip of our second Bloody Mary.

"Some things never change," Terry said, gratefully. Fortunately for her she could still go to Musso's without everyone dropping dead for her autograph. She wasn't *that* famous.

"You know," she said, leaning her perfect chin on her dainty palm, "I hate friends who die, too."

"Huh?"

"In that piece you wrote. The one I just read where you were talking about that friend of yours who died from heroin. I had a friend who O.D.ed too. From heroin. Two years ago."

"Oh, that story," I said.

"I was so mad. I hated it. I called up this guy I knew and had him bring some over and I shot up, right in the ass. I thought, shit, man! She's dead and I don't even know why!"

"But you can't," I said. "And besides, it's dangerous. Untrustworthy."

"Sure is great though."

"You're not still taking it are you?" I felt afraid. I was just beginning to feel something about her and now it turned out she might do herself in.

"No. I stopped a year and a half ago. But I think about it. Especially lately. All the time."

Having something that both kills pain *and* is illegal is too tempting when you've suddenly got everything but the prince, especially if you're an American. If they made it legal and you could just buy it, perhaps women would discover that heroin isn't what they need either.

At just that point, there was a frozen moment. Terry's gold and silver face seemed stopped in time, a stricken tinge around her mouth as she remembered; the new reddish-violet eye shadow brought out the baby's feet in her cheeks. Her luminous skin glowed.

All was silent, as the face of this heroine clearly revealed its tragic flaw.

I don't know how this story ends. I'm sort of hoping that because it's set in Los Angeles, the usual process will reverse itself in an L.A. double flip. An L.A. change. It would be very L.A. for Terry to decide to invent a success without the pain and fear: the burnt cloth and rancid gardenias. It would be nice if for some reason she decides to melt fame's lethal American power by getting some friends before it's too late and there's no one to talk to while she waits for the prince. And has nothing to do, like Janis Joplin did, but kill time.

# SIROCCO

*God what a night. I was so glad you were home, standing up in all that wind while everyone else was blowing across the streets like tumbleweeds. I wonder if you wish you hadn't been there, with the future looming up in such utter chaos before us. And meanwhile, the night was old and you were beautiful.*

A LONG time ago my mother and I were driving to a wedding. I had been engaged to both the groom and the best man at one time or another. I was twenty-three, a clerk-typist by day and a groupie-adventuress prowling the hot Sunset Strip at night. I'd broken off with both of those guys because I was impatient with ordinary sunsets; I was sure that somewhere a grandiose carnival was going on in the sky and I was missing it. But still, it made me feel funny having those guys slip away like that. "I wonder," I said to my mother, "if I'll ever get married."

"Well, if you do," she said, "marry someone you don't mind."

The only other piece of advice she gave me on the subject was to tell me that because I loved garlic so much I had better marry an Italian. "Or someone, dear, who likes garlic as much as you do."

Over the years I not only gave up the idea of finding an Italian I didn't mind, I gave up the idea of finding *any*one I didn't mind. But I was still sure there was a grandiose golden sunset somewhere in the sky.

When I was twenty-eight, I decided to make serious stabs at adulthood, and I plunged into fatal misadventures which nearly killed the poor men because all I did was spend their money, vamp the landscape, cry, and say, "I *hate* San Francisco." (Both of these serious stabs had a lot to do with San Francisco. All my adult-type bouts with reality take place there and always will.) After my second K.O., I packed everything I owned back in my car and drove south, back to L.A., knowing that I was never going to grow up like you're supposed to. I was almost thirty the late afternoon I finally got home to my town, and in the west an enormous luscious smoggy sunset cast itself in the air. My sister, who'd driven down with me, had told me unbelievably sordid tales about her trip to Hawaii in a thirty-six-foot sailboat that had taken six rather than three weeks to cruise, and how it had rained every single day. "One night when I was on watch," she told me, "it was real light because of the moon and there were huge swells, and then all of a sudden there was this white shark, as long as the boat, right beside me." (Within a month she forgot the entire bad part and now looks back with fondness upon the whole terrible journey.) But as foolhardy and dangerous as her trip had been, it was nothing compared to the man I'd picked as my adult male companion—a mean Texas Scorpio who would have shot me as soon as look at me, if he hadn't been so drunk he couldn't see. I courted disaster by casting aspersions on his thing about Sam Peckinpah ("You and Sam Peckinpah," I'd snarl, "are both eleven-and-a-half years old!"). For some reason, telling each other about what we'd been doing made me and my sister laugh so hard we had to pull off the road. Joy tingled through my eyes when I saw us glide past the L.A. city limits. Oh god, I thought, home.

Driving home, with my back against the giant orange bat of a sunset, east on Olympic Blvd. in the rush hour, I decided enough was enough, I would be satisfied with just the sunsets in Los Angeles and forget finding the someone I didn't mind.

I had a collection of lovers to keep me warm and my friendships with women, who always fascinated me by their wit, bravery, and resourcefulness, and who never told you the same story twice. Now, women I didn't mind. I mean, you can go places with a woman and come back just fine (or as my agent, Erica, plowed right in and said: "You know that when you have dinner with a girlfriend, you're going to come home a whole human being"). I had a third collection of associates who were men but not lovers. "Just friends," they're called. An American distinction if ever there was one. Only *we* would say "just" about a friend. My "just friends" were more reliable than most of my "just lovers," since "just lovers" were always capable of saying,

"Gee, you're puttin' on weight," or "Are *those* the shoes you're wearing?"

For over a year William was my closest "just friend." He lived not half a mile from me and was a free-lance writer, so we both got invited to the same sort of things to which it was assumed you'd take a presentable member of the opposite sex. (Terry Finch and I have glossed over this rule lately, and when they invite her to some local function and say bring "someone," she brings me.) Since my decision on Olympic Blvd. to give up on finding someone I didn't mind, I'd become much more resigned to lackluster events, or going with a "just friend." Before, I'd always gone everywhere alone.

Being places alone makes you think. Being there with someone makes you hounded by details, like what time the other person wants to leave; details that drain energy when you are trying to discover the core of an event. Being there with William put a damper on glorious possibilities. But I'd given up on those, which was why, I suppose, I went so many places with William.

Together, we covered the entire strata of L.A.-type events; we went to press parties, museum functions, art openings, dinners, screenings, and we even went places together when we didn't have to, like out to dinner. It was a passionless lethargy that bound me to him.

Less and less was I struck with the compromise I'd made, and pretty soon it looked just like real life.

It would have been more like me to hit the rough trade at Tana's, where potential lovers say, "*Now* what have you done to your hair?" Tana's is where everyone picks each other up and eats garlic. (It's weird to have a mother who is right even in specific details.) Tana's, with its quaint red and white tablecloths, its spinach salads, and the drunken endless waits for tables. Tana's is where I should have gone. Alone.

It seemed that all my lovers had but to whisper, "I have to catch a plane out of here in the morning..." and I was theirs. Sometimes they'd stay away for months and William and I could grow further and further into our pose. Sometimes my lovers would all descend from the sky at once, and William would frown at me for forgetting we'd been invited somewhere. I deserted William for my "just lovers" the way Gloria Steinem says women are not to desert women just because a man shows up.

William had lovers too, lots, and sometimes he would go off for a week or two into romantic heavens which made me shake my head. How could he still believe all that stuff, I used to ask him.

In the beginning, when we first became "just friends," William used to stare at me wistfully, waiting for me to get crazed or drunk enough to fall into bed with him. But I never got that drunk or that crazed, and finally William put aside his romantic dreams about me, the way I'd abandoned mine the afternoon I came home from San Francisco for the very last time. The very last time.

And everything would have stayed that way, too, if it hadn't been for the sirocco, even though I hate blaming things on the weather.

It was one of those nights when the Santa Anas were blowing so hard that searchlights were the only things in the sky that were straight. From earliest childhood I have rejoiced over the Santa Ana winds. My sister and I used to run outside and dance under the stars on our cool front lawn and laugh manically and sing "Hitch-hike, hitch-hike, give us a ride," imagining we could be taken up into the sky on broomsticks. Raymond Chandler and Joan Didion both regard the Santa Anas as some powerful evil, and I know what they mean because I've seen people drop from migraines and go crazy. Every time *I* feel one coming, I put on my dancing spirits.

Once, when I was fifteen, I walked for an entire afternoon along the empty cement in 110 degrees of hot dry winds just to get the feel of them, alone. Everyone else was hiding inside.

I know those winds the way Eskimos know their snows.

William and I were together as usual, attending the opening of a new club called the Blue Champagne. The confusion, the roly-poly of the winds made me hilarious. Nothing can keep me sober when everything is flapping around for dear life. They were trying to have a rather dignified opening with red-coated parking-lot attendants and nothing would stay put or straight, except, of course, the pattern of the searchlights crisscrossing the sky.

We ran into a discarded lover of mine, Jack, who was trying to ignore me, but his girlfriend's hat blew across the entrance and I caught it, so he was stuck having to be grateful. The girlfriend suggested we all sit together. She was either completely in, or totally out, of fashion, I thought; her clothes were so her own. She introduced herself as Isabella Farfalla and shook my hand. Jack followed her in, wishing we weren't all going to sit together.

The champagne (which was not blue) was free, and we wound up drinking four bottles of it. I also, it seems, wound up madly embracing Isabella Farfalla.

"Oh, *no*," I cried to William, who telephoned the next morning to rub it in. "I thought it was a dream!"

"That's the second one of Jack's you've taken away from him..." William said, amused.

"Huh?"

"Wasn't Shawn going with him when you..." he reminded.

And of course, then I remembered back when Jack had had a mad crush on this elegantly handsome but ambivalent young man named Shawn. Shawn lumped all love together and was drawn to whatever burned hottest, which is usually me. So not only had I abandoned Jack, but I'd run off with what he'd rather have had in the first place: Shawn. Shawn's and my romance was faint to begin with and faded away altogether when he went home to Charleston for a month. Anyway, he'd been "just a lover" so I had hardly noticed. And besides, I thought that whole sector of society Jack was in was flimsy because no one had any real style: They had Porsches and were skinny and took cocaine and weren't even in the movie business— they were all in peripheral situations like advertising and magazines. Lots of art directors. (The only good art director is a retired art director.)

"You two really looked beautiful," William sighed about me and Isabella, "kissing each other like that."

"Well. At least we looked beautiful," I said. "*Now* what do I do?"

"Maybe you really like women better," he suggested. "Maybe that's been it all along."

"But what does one *do* with women?" I said, imagining at once exactly what one would do. "It was probably just the Santa Ana," I said.

"You never kissed *me* like that," he replied.

You know, when you come to think about it, it's a wonder women have anything to do with men at all, and no surprise that men have devised all kinds of schemes to bind women to them, like not giving them any money. If you had your choice of sleeping with a beautiful soft creature or a large hard one, which would you pick? I mean, if they both had the same amount of money?

Isabella Farfalla, it turned out, was a beast of prey who descended upon unsuspecting women (who would suspect?), and before they knew it they'd be where I was, wondering, in the morning, what had happened. Not her, I said to myself, she might be dangerous.

A week later I saw her at a party, her black-jet bead eyes watching a nineteen-year-old girl across the room, waiting for the moment when the girl would have had just too much to drink.

Isabella Farfalla was from Perugia and made her living in Hollywood taking pictures of movie stars for a European wire service. She was bored with the ancient decadence that her own country provided and had come to L.A. because everything seemed so fresh. But Isabella was a devastating force who got bored with the pace and would liven things up just because it was her nature to interject chaos at the very time things had about ossified. She was like the Santa Anas, and if she hadn't kissed me, William and I would probably still be going to the museum together. Entombed.

For a month after that night, the weather was bland and dreary, plodding along on the strength of seventy-five-degree days and sixty-degree nights. The Midwest was hit by blizzards, the South by hurricanes, and the East by early winters.

William and I entered the winter season in our summer clothes.

We went to more art parties and took a lot of cocaine; cocaine being the drug of divorce and October being a divorce month since people want to get it over with before the holidays.

But things had changed between me and William. Changed back. He'd begun to look at me with renewed romance and I'd catch him across crowded rooms. What was so odd was that women actually thought he was sexy. To please him, they brought me presents.

"What's this for?" I wondered when the first woman shyly presented me with an antique cigarette box, the night after she'd slept with William.

"I just thought you might . . . like it," she said.

I looked at William, his dashing cossack-sort of appearance so impossible to imagine naked beside me. It wasn't the way he looked that made him impossible. It was what he said. It was his sense of humor. He *would* not resist a pun. And any man who will not resist a pun will never lie up-pun me. William was lacking in some major essential that made passion impossible, but he still looked at me and I'd catch him in the shadows, staring, while some lithe, smiling girl followed his gaze and either gave up or decided to "understand" and give me another present.

I had a box full of silk roses, cigarette cases, crystal beads, and earrings by the beginning of October when the second Santa Ana struck.

It was a Sunday and the Santa Ana had been afoot since the night before. It was so dry that bougainvillea, picked, would embalm in the heat and last forever like Japanese paper flowers. Day Tully, the most beautiful girl in the world, had telephoned me in a vacant hope that I might know of something to spark her up—she'd even been unable to read, she complained; she'd spent all morning in a cold tub, and what did people *do* out here (she was from Seattle) when it was like this? "Come over," I suggested.

Even sere from the winds, Day Tully had the matter-of-fact face of a 1948 calendar girl for farmers. She was America-for-spacious-skies, the reason our boys died gladly in the war. She was an actress, and like all actresses, she was only real when she was pretending. One of her favorite pretenses was the part of a bright young actress interested in all the arts, but especially writing. In fact, she'd never even read *Pride and Prejudice* or *Catch-22*.

She looked at me with the bedazzled adoration of a young boy flung on the sands of a hopeless crush. Because I was a writer, she said. Her brown hair crackled from the lightning in the air and she kept trying to pin it back with a blue barrette but it wouldn't stay.

"Let's walk to William's," I said. "I like to walk when it's like this."

"O.K.," she said, "but I hear this wind changes people into maniacs."

William was glad to see us since he grows scattered in the winds and can't concentrate. He poured out three freezing-cold, green jigger glasses of vodka and we toasted each other and drank. Before she put her drink down, Day explained that she really wasn't a drinker, but William and I were, and we would have none of it.

It was probably when I began to help her with her blue barrette... Anyway, William claimed afterward that I was the first to pounce. What I wouldn't do with Isabella, who knew what she was doing, I now smoothly instigated between Day and William and myself. Passion from boredom and vodka flashed through my veins, passion and fanned curiosity toppled us, Santa Ana-ed, down upon William's bed. Only not William. I wouldn't let William touch me, and we almost tore poor Day in half.

If William couldn't ever have me, then he at least had what I wanted, because in the end, Day, like those other women, actually fell in love with him. By the end of the afternoon, she was hooked.

We stood in front of William's apartment in the twilight heat and Day drunkenly implored me to come with "us." She and William had suddenly become "us," and I had a nasty vision of William finally meeting someone who'd listen to his poetry and think he was a great writer. And I was so drunk I said, "William is a *dumb* writer! He's not...interesting."

I left them in front of William's apartment, ablaze with confusion and determined to *do* something. Talk to someone. The only person who knew anything about this stuff was Shawn, who, thank god, was home and receiving and always sober.

He was listening to Chopin and putting lighter fluid in a cigarette lighter that looked like it weighed twelve pounds and was made out of bronze. It had figurines waltzing on it, a man and a woman, since it was also a music box, not just a lighter. He was wearing a silver silk kimono that must have come from Charleston since it was certainly not L.A., and all his windows were open, which blew the room around slightly. He was just beautiful.

It is a Hollywood tale that Shawn's heart was broken in Charleston by a charming aging millionaire named Mark, who suddenly, after eight years of seamless happiness, decided to grab every young boy there was. Except Shawn. Shawn had left his Mercedes, his mink-lined trench coat, his silver rooms in Charleston, and come to Hollywood with no family in the business and no experience but charm and a determination to please at all costs. The odd thing about Shawn was that I really didn't mind him. I didn't mind his broken life or bygone silver tassels or Mark. I told him my version of the afternoon and ended with "How *could* she, Shawn, have gone with William when *I* wanted her?"

"You probably scared her to death," he pointed out. "You do that a lot, you know."

"But then, how could William ...?"

"Sometimes if you can't get what you want, you get what the person you want wants." He blew at the wick of the lighter and held up the dancers, who were now polished. "I don't know how you can spend all that time with William anyway, he's such a goon."

"Oh," I said automatically, "we're 'just friends.'"

After that night, though, those male "just friends" melted away. William and Day tried to include me in their romance; Day especially tried to, but I already had enough cigarette cases for someone who doesn't even smoke.

Isabella had gone off to Italy for a while and when she returned, Shawn and I ran into her several times. Overwhelmed by naked curiosity, she came by my apartment one afternoon and asked me how it had happened that I'd broken up with a real man like William and was now seen everywhere with someone as obviously gay as Shawn, and didn't I miss sex, or what?

"He's not that gay," I explained, "and besides we have fun."

"I don't get it," she persisted. "People are really wondering about you two—all the time—together."

"God, people..." I said.

The thing is now that when I'm with Shawn I don't even *care* if there's some grandiose carnival in the sky I might be missing. Just think, if we didn't have the Santa Anas, how straight we all would be. Like the patterns of those searchlights outside the Blue Champagne.

# RAIN

WHEN YOU feel as though you can't stand it another moment, that you'd rather be living in Siberia than go through another bleak stretch of parking-lot days and smog—that you might *even* reexamine the possibility of San Francisco, where the view of the bay will always be before you in constant testimony to your adult wisdom—when all that happens, it *still* doesn't rain.

If only it would rain—just rain. Each morning Shawn looks at the ceiling, and the color of his room is just how it was in Charleston on a morning when it was raining outside.

"Is it raining?" he'd ask.

"Oh, of course not," I would say, and I, nearer the window, would see the Hollywood sign in high relief, portending plain heat. "Not only is it not raining," I would say, "but I think it's going to be ninety again today."

"Ninety?" It would cheer him. He loves heat.

But it didn't cheer me.

The rain is freedom; it has always been like that in L.A. It's freedom from smog and unbroken dreary hateful sameness, it's freedom to look out the window and think of London and little violets and Paris and cobblestones. It's freedom to be cozy. Cozy! You can be cozy and not even have to go to San Francisco.

My favorite rain of all was in Rome where it came down in uncompromising wetness and everything got All Wet. You'd sit inside your pensione room, which was likely to be in a nice Renaissance castle, and you'd think, my god, for centuries these people have been moping around these gigantic rooms in the cold, with cold marble floors and no fireplaces, wondering what was for dinner. And Italians, I've noticed, never drink the way we do. They play bridge. So other sterner nations say "sunny Italy," and "Italians are such children," when in truth it's not sunny and it's a toss-up as to who are the more childish, the Germans, singing in bars in German with their arms around each other, or Italians, playing bridge, gossiping, and wondering what's for dinner. I spent six months in Italy and it rained for five of them and oh! it was just heaven.

The rain in Mexico, that humid rain-jungle kind of rain with flashy colors and limes and the idea that if you got jungle rot, the tentacles of the carnivorous vines would cover you up, dead—that Mexican rain, I have to think twice about. I have tried to love all rain, but I don't know about jungle rain. The tropics are not for me. Birds with flaming plumage and fruits with neon-pink centers in the rain—I bet if I had to have even two unbroken days of that, I'd slip right out of my mind the way that missionary did over Sadie Thompson. I'd rather just be Sadie Thompson and get it over with, but I'm afraid I'd turn into a Calvinist in hot rain, with transparent underlying motives and a worm-eaten, jungle-rotted Bible as my brain's downfall.


The morning after the sirocco when I wound up at Shawn's and William and Day were left to live happily ever after, L.A. lay once more beneath a leaden sky. Birds poised motionless, halfway between destination and home. Beds were left unmade; no one could untwist their sheets with "earthquake weather" breathing down our necks.

I met my sister for lunch at Ports but the lethargy was so universal that neither of us could decide what we wanted or even if we were hungry. We ordered two bottles of Mexican mineral water called Agua Tehuacan. It comes in clear glass bottles with a silver label depicting a humid landscape, a few orange and Tijuana-green palm trees, a silver bay, a silver frame around it all. Ports serves this mineral water in brandy snifters with lots of ice and a slice of lime. The bottle is left beside your glass to satisfy visual cravings, which were, it turned out, the only ones in evidence. We weren't hungry and ordered nothing else. Inside Ports you could forget a lot of things; it had the atmosphere of a colonial outpost. But outside the afternoon was lethal: No sunglasses could cut the glare, and even your pores shrank back against the light.

When I got home, a friend from New York telephoned.

"What's wrong?" she asked.

"The weather," I said.

"The weather! Are you kidding? It's been raining now for two weeks and you talk about weather. I can read the papers—it's wonderful out in California. What weather?"

"The light!" I explain.

"God, you kids out there are really the end," she says. "The *light*!"

Outside, the streets were suffocated beneath stagnant pressure. Humans moved from here to there with queer carelessness and you could not drive down a residential street without someone backing straight out of their driveway in front of you as though the world were empty.

On the weekend following the night I wound up at Shawn's, we drove down to Laguna and stayed with some friends of his. Coming back on the freeway Sunday night, it was almost as though our weekend had never existed: Shawn lost his temper (I didn't even know he had one) at the traffic and all the way back in the car he told me about how great Mark was, how charming and splendid.

I wondered why he'd chosen that time to speak of Mark, since the calm ocean pull might still be caressing us had Shawn shut up. But now, all of a sudden he was angry at traffic and just everything.

Long ago I used to talk to my lovers about Graham as though to keep the truth before us, and I had supposed that that was what Shawn was doing, lest we forget that reality lay with Mark and not with what Shawn and I had managed to come up with—the peace. The peace, it seemed, counted for nothing. It was Mark and his endless parties, his spectacular dinners, and private planes, and old money that meant something. Poor Shawn's a fool, I thought to myself, remembering the look of perfect rapture that comes upon him whenever he sees the ocean. Poor Shawn thinks he likes silver rooms and gay Southern adventures when he really likes to lie in the sand.

"You know," Shawn was saying, "if you came to Charleston, Mark would have a great big party for you."

"I don't like great big parties," I said. "I like lying down with you." It seemed to me that Shawn was possessed by the Angel of Sex more and more. He was approaching my ideal in record time and even Graham was beginning to pale by comparison.

The funny thing was that I'd always believed that sex master-pieces were the best kind. Better than Bach, the Empire State Build-ing, or Marcel Proust. I believe that most people put ninety-eight percent of all their creative energy into trying to stage marvelous love scenes. I believe that adultery is an art form. In France, they more or less lay their cards on the table and ennoble love affairs for the creative adventures they are, because for most people, these are the *only* creative adventures they'll ever have. The *only* chance they'll ever get to touch the face of heaven.

"You know," Shawn said, "during the last couple of years I was with Mark, I stopped sleeping with him."

"Why?"

"Because," he said. The downtown traffic was floundering.

"Was it because he started the young-boy routine?" I asked.

"No. It was me. I just didn't want to do it anymore..." he said. "He wanted us to get a big old house and have every queen in the South over for dinner."

"Well..." I said. "But *why* didn't you sleep with him?"

"I just...didn't," he said. "In fact, for the last year and a half, since after that first time with you, I've been thinking the sex part of my life was over."

"Forever?" I wondered. (What about *me*?!)

"Except for you," he said. "I just never felt like being with any-one."

"Well," I said, "any fool can want to sleep with *me*. I mean, look at me, the only thing one *can* think about me is sex."

The truth is that when you're as voluptuous and un-hair-sprayed as I am, you have to cover yourself in un-ironed muumuus to walk to the corner and mail a letter. Men take one look and start calculating how they can get rid of obstacles and where the closest bed would be. This all happens in spite of my many serious flaws and imperfections, in spite of my being much too fat and everyone else being just right. The reason for this is because my skin is so healthy it radiates its own kind of moral laws; people simply cannot resist being attracted to what looks like pure health. Whoever is in charge of everything doesn't want the survival of the fittest to come about just from wars and famine; whoever's in charge also fixed it so people would just naturally opt for health. (In fact, without rouge I am nothing. It's called "Shading Rouge," it only comes in one color, it's by Evelyn Marshall, and it makes most people look like they've just stepped out of an English landscape one hundred years ago.) I also have nearly perfect teeth, which I believe is the real secret to the universe. Nice teeth, flashing out of even a pock-marked face, equal survival of the species. I know you never think of nice bones pulsing away in clean, healthy calcium, but some inner conclusion is jumped to by people who see nice teeth. Anyway, any fool can want to sleep with me; it doesn't take a genius. Even Shawn couldn't resist.

"I know how men look at you," Shawn said. "Some of them look at me the same way."

"*I* look at you that way," I said. "Although I try not to be too oafish."

The first time I saw Shawn without his clothes on I felt as astonished as Actaeon coming across Diana naked in the woods, bathing. That is how beautiful he was. Only I wasn't shocked merely because he was a Greek god whom you weren't supposed to see naked, I was struck because he *looked* like a Greek god. And not just a simple classical perfection which leaves the viewer detached from the marvels of the human body but makes one yearn for the real life of Clark Gable's wink. Shawn, when he first took off his clothes in front of me and I saw him standing there, *there*—in my very own bedroom, my very own St. Sebastian—caused me to gasp and say, "Jesus Christ, Shawn, look at how gorgeous you are!" He was grace under pressure the way I never have been when men have said similar things to me. After that I wondered why I got so angry at men who said dumb things when they saw something they thought was beautiful.

But now it hadn't rained in so long that coming into L.A. in that dense quicksand traffic made all the green water in Laguna subside into quicksand smog. Laguna with its emerald bay could have just been a fragment of a dream for all the thirst for heaven it slaked. Shawn would not stop talking about Mark, and it was too much trouble for me to dredge up Graham stories as subtle object lessons because Shawn never got anything that was subtle. No men do. At least, not around me.

This cloud, I prayed, has simply *got* to have a silver lining.


The silver lining was rain. A sudden, mistaken rain that came all at once in the middle of the following Thursday, vanishing after five minutes upon noticing its blunder. No clouds, seventy-five degrees, no reason, but it rained. It rained on the hot oily asphalt and made it smell rainy. It rained the gray from the landscape, just like that, with a snap of its wrong turn.

The wild blue yonder came upon us like a drunken zoom lens thundering into focus. It seemed that God had made up His mind to change the background without telling anyone.

Los Angeles got huge shafts of pure yellow sunlight surging through office windows. Daffodils came to mind. Violets.

You could choose any direction and see as far as you wanted. Past Catalina and on west all the way to the East. In a quick clap of mistaken thunder the look of Southern California had been transformed miraculously and I have seen nothing like it anywhere else or heard of any such thing.

You could pick up mad gladness from bus drivers and studio chiefs and pool cleaners and check-out girls and guys doing the news on the radio. "Rain!" they cried, and immediately meteorologists were contacted to predict more rain. Rain from Mexico, rain from the San Joaquin Valley, rain from a storm out in the Pacific, rain coming down from Oregon. Converging rain—we're *bound* to have more rain.

"Did you see it, it rained!" everyone said to each other, in soft panting voices as though they were in love.

Ports takes to rain oddly. When Ports opened, the first day I ever went there, it was raining outside and I fell in love with the place. The name, the odd food, the sneaky private room with a small strange library filled with Max Beerbohm and Ford Madox Ford, it all looked like *my* restaurant. My very own. It was comfortable and clubby in a very snotty English colonial beat-the-natives-if-you-catch-them-stealing but deal-out-prodigious-kindness-for-loyalty way. I thought to myself, I have *got* to get into *this* movie.

Olivia and Frank, the married owners, had opened the restaurant because, Frank said, "We want this to be a workers' café." "Workers" however, took one look and asked what had happened to Ernie, the guy who used to run the beer bar there. And anyway, Frank basically loathes "workers" and within a month was snarling at one of his waiters, "How dare you enter a formal dining room with your jacket unbuttoned; you're fired!" But that first day Frank was in the kitchen being the chef. Olivia was having to be the waitress, which turned her into a hummingbird of naked nerve endings—she spilled everything. It made you hysterical to watch her, so I volunteered to pour wine and the next thing you know I was being a waitress for three months for free.

I loved it more than anything I've ever done before or since because deep down inside every woman is a waitress. The act of waitressing is a solace, it's got everything you could ask for—confusion, panic, humility, and food.

It was in those early days, when Ports got written up by Lois Dwan in the *L.A. Times*, that I first noticed that rain jammed Ports. People would not take no for an answer. They'd open the door and see all those bodies crammed together like the subway at 5:15 but no! they were determined, they didn't care, it was raining outside, and the only place to be when it rained was Ports, and that was all there was to it. In Los Angeles rain is such a special occasion that to savor it fully you must match it up with the right crazy place.

In those days Ports was only open for lunch. I'd arrive at 11:30 and Olivia and I would huddle together over coffee awaiting the deluge and trading Valium. By about 3:00, we would go through a ritual of apologies with Frank, eat our lunch, and wonder if an irate producer would ever come back after having to wait an hour and a half for milk and a chicken salad. "Well," Olivia would say with high-strung contempt, "ordering milk! Really!"


"It's raining!" I telephoned Shawn. "Let's go to Ports tonight."

"Raining!?" He sounded asleep. "I've been editing slides all day. Is it really raining?"

"Yes!" I said. "Let's *do* something!"

"Yeah, but Ports..." he said. Shawn had once volunteered to be a waiter at Ports and it had nearly killed him; his central nervous system is incapable of free-form madness. Overseeing three hundred extras was child's play for Shawn after working nights at Ports.

When they opened Ports up at night, the place really staged some remarkable magic acts: Ibsen dramas and high farce, but you never knew when and sometimes they overlapped. Romantic tension was one of the major underlying pulses of Ports at night. I thought that going there with Shawn with the rain outside would be an opportunity for high art, if you believe, as I do, that sex is art.

"Well..." he said. "O.K. Let's go to Ports."

"I'll come over," I said. "I have something for you."

It drizzled all afternoon and was just beginning to rain a little harder that night as I started off to Shawn's in a giddy bubble of damp expectations. The other cars on Santa Monica were careful, for as the water hits the streets for the first time in ages, all the oil is dissolved and radio warnings about freeway skids and pile-ups and death are the second thing they tell you, once they establish that it is raining.

I had two Quaaludes, Shawn's favorite drug. They are the only

substance I've ever taken that could live up to a reputation as an aphrodisiac. Shawn calls them quackers. They went with the rain.

Quaaludes, taken circumspectly (which is their whole problem because the moment people find out that by god this is an aphrodisiac
that actually *works*, they start cramming them wholesale down their
throats. Quaaludes reverse your peristalsis and you wind up choking
to death on your own vomit like Jimi Hendrix because they make
your body *too* relaxed and you don't want to be *that* relaxed)...uh,
Quaaludes, taken circumspectly, are just wonderful for those nice
Sunday lay-abouts, or even, if you take just a quarter of one, a night
on the town. You'll end up dancing and having a wonderful time in
a very relaxed way, a way so relaxed that you forget to drink, and the
next morning you wake up and you've actually lost a couple of pounds
and gained some exercise. I could go on and on about Quaaludes,
but the medical profession would probably get huffy, what with so
many of their women patients becoming addicted to them, before
the F.D.A. could figure out that a lot of car accidents seemed to in-
volve about forty quackers found in the purse of the driver. They are
dangerous. But they are made for sex and sex is our art.

They do two other things. They make you tell everything, with
no reservations, everything (like the time I told Shawn about how,
when I was four, I tried to set my sister on fire). And they are a contact aphrodisiac, unlike other hypnotics. When *you* get very languid
and sexual and smile like Cleopatra being fanned as she floats down
the Nile, other people catch the mood and find themselves straying
from the straight and narrow too.

With Shawn and me as a couple, out in society on a quarter of a
Quaalude apiece, a kind of irresistible pull develops. People take us
aside and say things like, "You two have the secret of life." Or they
look at us fondly and say, "You really do know how to love each
other." Passion ornamented with chemistry.

That night of the hard sirocco, when I'd arrived on Shawn's door-
step, disheveled and miserable, at the end of my rope and without
even my "just friend" William to count on, Shawn had put me into
his bed under his light silk kimono and told me not to worry, that

stranger things had happened than me and Day and William. That was why I'd gone over to Shawn's in the first place, to hear that. People, he continued, lived through a lot weirder combinations but what had really struck him the next day when he thought about it was that the symmetry was all wrong. "It was unbalanced," Shawn said, "and that's why it made you feel bad.

"You are perfect for Los Angeles, you know. You're like the lady whom everyone's in love with but they hate themselves for it because you're all wrong. They don't have anything to go on with you. No precedents. You're voluptuous and too smart and too kind and too mean, and you give everyone just what they want and then you get sad and bland...I used to wonder why you dressed the way you did—one minute I see you in those old shirts and that scarf!...and the next you're at some art thing and I see women look at you when you don't know it and they're all wondering how in the hell you *did* it. You glow."

Shawn is one of the few men on earth who does not take the opportunity to kick you when you're down. He makes your faults sound like the inevitable by-products of how brilliant you are. And for the very first time in my life, I began to deep-down know that even though I was not as thin as George Harrison, it was going to be all right. In fact, it might even be funny.

I remember when I first started having lovers, they never failed to remind me that if I didn't watch out, I'd get *really* fat (implying that I was painful enough to behold as it was). Then the Beatles came with their Jane Ashers and those Mary Quant clothes that you could only wear if you were ten years old and raised on English cabbage. For about five years all my conversations with women were about diets; they always zeroed in on the pivotal reality of their life, which was that they were imperfect. Not like George Harrison. But with me, especially, I was doomed to have this flesh all over me, unless I ate only vegetables and fish and drank only Perrier water, I practiced my yoga faithfully, I never forgot to drink apple cider vinegar and take kelp pills; if I did all of that—why then, there I'd be in a room and you wouldn't be able to tell me apart from all the other women who were clawing with their fingernails to maintain the same size. It's a horrible paradox.

When Shawn, the morning after the sirocco, gave me his well-considered and carefully prepared little speech I thought, Maybe he's right. It couldn't hurt to *think* I was beautiful anyway. After all, I think L.A.'s beautiful and it's not fashionable or right.

The very next night I was having dinner with this fashionable young rich man who looked at me as I smoothed some paté over some toast and said, "You better watch out with that stuff. It'll make you fat."

"Well, gee," I said to him, "there are so many perfect women, it's just horrible you have to spend time sitting here with me."

Arrogance and conceit and remarks like that one are much more fun than starving all the time. Once it is established that you are you and everyone else is merely perfect, ordinarily factory-like perfect... you can wreak all the havoc you want.

There is something fascinating about a person's face when they're not falling apart because of their imperfections and self-loathing. Pleasure is a lure. When you're smiling, the whole world would rather smile with you and have another watercress sandwich than ponder the universe with an ex-Beatle. The first time I began to realize all this was with Shawn the night it finally rained. It became clear to me that beauty has nothing to do with fashion, that love can conquer anything, sex is art, and let's see... hope springs eternal. I love the rain.

It seemed to me as we drove down Santa Monica with the liquor-store lights all halos of color that Shawn was enhanced in such a blurry, silver fox of a night. So charming, I thought as the Quaalude came on, it's all so charming. I felt like a floppy, prize-winning iris, content to be an iris, all lavender and silken, the kind they call True Blue.

We parked outside Ports; there was a spot almost in front to emphasize our right living. Inside I greeted Olivia and Frank as we took off our coats, and there was Ports, overflowing with all sorts of people who can't resist when it's raining.

The jukebox played Argentine tangos to remind everyone of passion.

"Aren't they beautiful?" Olivia asked me about a tall bunch of white irises. "Sally brought them!"

"Yes, they're just gorgeous," I said. "Now." (Olivia's favorite joke was one that a friend of hers used to exclaim upon seeing Olivia's three-day-old bouquets: "Oh! How lovely those must have been.")

Shawn and I were induced to sit with a table full of designers. L.A. is loaded with designers, art directors, and representatives from amazing Milanese furniture manufacturers. These people don't live in apartments like most people, or studios like artists; they live in "spaces." "How do you like my space?" they ask, showing you some inconceivable, uncozy, anti-Dickens ode to white, chrome, and inch-thick glass.

"But where do you sleep?" I wonder, nervous.

"There's a space up those stairs," I'm told.

"But those stairs…I mean, those stairs don't have banisters. Aren't you afraid of falling head first on your coffee table and wrecking the glass? The glass looks pretty expensive."

But designers never get looped enough to get blood on their spaces. Red doesn't go with the white and chrome. (Not that they necessarily have red blood, come to think of it.)

I exclude Italians from all this because somehow when Italians do it, it's human and O.K. Italians would never live in a "space" because "spaces" are likely to cast eerie glows over dinner parties from too much white. No Italian would brook that sort of nonsense at dinner.

Half the people at the table were Italians and the other half were trying to become Italian by osmosis: tutored in the language, all Italian friends, all Italian furniture. The non-Italians would never have chosen to go to Ports; the Italians were the ones who insisted, because they were charmed by a place that was so "Inglese," or "So like thees marvelous Inglese writer—D. H. Lawrence!" (All the fancy Italians I know who come to America make sure they go to Taos because of D. H. Lawrence.)

Among the non-Italians was a killer tar-baby named Al Stills. I'd never known what a tar-baby was until Shawn explained one after-noon in Laguna that a tar-baby is one of those people who drive you crazy through your life by never responding to anything you do no matter what kind of display you cook up for their delight. And the more you try to embrace your tar-baby, the more you get stuck in the tar and the worse everything is. Jim Morrison was one of my tar-babies, and I see now (that it's too late) that he could have been a dear sweet friend, even a lover, if I hadn't created from the very be-ginning the seeds of tar-babydom. Al Stills had never been one of my tar-babies, but I noticed that a lot of people in Los Angeles were just fascinated by him and terrified at the same time. He had a clean, Icelandic brilliance that floored people in L.A. And he never said too much, he always smiled nicely (white, white teeth), and was not too smart. It must have been his basic mediocre brain that drew people to him; he was like an animal who's too much of an animal to comprehend the inevitability of his own death, and that kind of per-son is always a comfort.

The funny thing, the great part about it, was that Al Stills had a worse tar-baby than anyone—Italy. He would have done anything to make Italy notice him, he worshiped her with all his might. But she, of course, has always ignored Icelandic northerners. And so it is that she has drawn blonds with ice-blue eyes to Venice with its Grand Canal and flamboyant history, while Italians are always wandering off to New Mexico, seeking an empty past. I loathe adobe so I've never gone to the desert with any Italians, but I can imagine they just love all that dirt with nothing on it. (The idea of trying to "find your-self" in some kind of geographical illusion is enough to make me so disgusted and bored that I am likely to get nasty. Although I see now that my trips to San Francisco must be more than meets the eye.)

Italy, my love, my own, has never been a tar-baby to me. It's always loved me back; it let me go; we had a very simple passion for each other which was amoral and beyond jealousy.

Perhaps what I have lets me take Italy for granted and think, Well of *course* the buildings are more beautiful here, of *course* the shoes are better, of *course* the gas stations are sonnets of miraculous design . . . and, thinking that, come home to L.A. Because you don't love things just because they're beautifully designed; you appreciate them and go home. Maybe the reason I don't get stuck on Italy is that I'm so jaded—that a girlhood beside the Pacific Ocean makes one accept perfection like arms and legs, without getting all tarred up. Simple tricks like rain are what get me.

Al Stills was a natural tar-baby for Shawn. Shawn just couldn't help it; it was built into his soul. Shawn from the falling-apart South, unpainted plantation mansions, moss, and slow, gentle men and women inviting "you all come back . . ." Poor Shawn could do nothing for Al Stills; Al Stills simply could not see Shawn. Oh, sometimes he would catch a ray of Shawn when he was told by an Italian that Shawn was one of the best designers around (Shawn was a natural-born knower of where things went). And then Al would smile and try to make small talk but Shawn would vanish in front of his face and he'd forget what he was saying.

We were all sitting at a big table, about five Italians and five others including Al Stills. Shawn was captured by two Italian women, which left me sitting next to Al Stills, who poured me wine and smiled his white, white smile.

The Argentine tangos sustained the background, although by this time we didn't need to be reminded of passion. Those Quaaludes made everything Argentine tangos. Especially Shawn with those eyes of his, that strange color gray. I raised my glass to him across the table. But now what was Al Stills saying . . . ?

"What are you *wear*ing?" he was asking, leaning toward me, almost touching my neck.

"Oh . . . perfume. Le De Givenchy. What I always wear," I said. It was a play so I moved slightly back. If he leaned still more toward me, then *I* was *his* tar-baby and life was a French farce.

He moved more toward me.


I can't think how we got Al Stills away from his Italians and over to Shawn's crowded, Charleston antebellum apartment at 2:00 a.m.

that rainy night, much less explain how we all three wound up in bed. I think it was something about a brandy. Al Stills wanted a brandy, I wanted to be with Shawn, Al Stills wanted to be with me *and* have this brandy, Shawn had brandy, and so . . . But then, how did we all get into bed together without ever drinking the brandy? It must have been those Quaaludes.

Shawn and I arrived first at Shawn's apartment and we were both perfectly sober when we came to some sort of unspoken understanding that poor Al Stills didn't stand a chance. I was going to hand Shawn his tar-baby on a silver mattress. But Al Stills must have known we were up to no good when he arrived at Shawn's a few minutes after we did and found me naked in bed and Shawn in his silver silk kimono.

That must have been the night Shawn and I fell in love, more or less. Perhaps the blond northerner drew us together under the roof where the slow rain fell. Poor Al Stills was very nice about it.

My mother once said that sex was only good if it was dirty and *verboten* and I've never found anything to disprove this. Shawn and Al Stills were both lapsed Catholics and you can't get dirtier or more *verboten* than that.

It was slightly awkward to find ourselves with a stranger in pursuit of the Holy Grail, and we tried to make things as nice as possible for him, just as he probably, in his heart, thought we were "such children." It was sort of marbleized, the North and the South, with the rain in the night outside. There was an elegance because of the rain.

And then somehow it was morning. A yellow shaft of light fell across our untouched brandy and there was Shawn looking down at me. He kissed me and whispered that he was going to take a shower and would be back, with coffee, soon.

All art fades but sex fades fastest. Poor Al Stills woke up with a hangover and groaned. "Oh god," he said, "you mean he's up already?"

"Yes," I said.

"I guess Shawn has always been on top of every situation," poor Al Stills said.

"I can't find the coffee," Shawn came in to say. "We could go to Sarno's."

It was just the thing. Sarno's is an Italian coffee bar and it would make Al Stills feel perfect. And indeed I could see a look of worldliness grace his face. He had survived a perilous adventure with dignity, and of course, Shawn had made it all look so easy, perfectly charming, as always.

I fell in love with Shawn more when he picked up the check for breakfast and insisted that it all was on him. *That's* when I fell in love with him, I remember now perfectly.

We parted back at Shawn's in bright sunlight. Al Stills went off to his "space" in his Ferrari; he waved to us as he drove past. Shawn pushed my bangs away from my eyes and said, "Let's go to Laguna next weekend. You want to?"

"Of course," I said. "Unless it rains."

Shawn watched Al Stills turn left and disappear. "You know," he said, "he didn't even...None of that made a bit of difference to him."

"For him this is just slumming, not real life at all. You know who he really likes? Isabella Farfalla, because she's so mean to him and Italian to boot," I said.

But even in L.A. it has to rain sometimes. It would never snow, it would never ever be so cold as to throw a blizzard on us. Italians may be "such children" but their tar-babies are not physical pain or coldness; they want an absence of history, they want to start fresh. When they designed those big palaces in Rome they must have known all along about hope and death, but they were so graceful they made it look easy.

# BAD DAY AT PALM SPRINGS

*Since both David and you promised to supply me with your own personal versions of this adventure, I've been expecting at least* something. *But neither of you has come up with a single morsel. Oh, every now and then David will say, "I'm really not so crazy. I mean, I try not to do things that make me really miserable. The only time I screwed up was that time in Palm Springs. God was that a piece of shit." And all* you *probably recall is how nice it was lying there naked in the sun (in front of three women, looking the way you do naked with your fucking cock making me really hope, my darling, that you'd get the sunburn you deserved. But no). Albee probably could have made something out of the ghastly assortment of people, but I would rather not think about theatrical possibilities, no matter how suitable that place would have been as a stage.*

WHEN I was a child my father never approved of Palm Springs; he said it was too expensive and we would drive right through to Indio. I liked Indio because the Woolworth's there had the same Japanese-made papoose tape-measure covers that were sold as curios all over the Great Southwest. Palm Springs was not considered part of that territory. But perhaps I am getting Indio mixed up with Taos, where, for one week, my father exposed the family to enough Southwest to last a lifetime.

We always went to the desert in Indio after that. My sister and I believed that you could spread your hand out on your thigh for fifteen minutes in the sun, and when you lifted it up, you'd have a handprint, the tans were so easy to get there.

When the desert became the place to go for Easter vacation–high school rampages, my father agreed to splurge and give me Palm Springs just once. I'd had a wisdom tooth removed the day before we went and hemorrhaged all week, my face half swollen and one eye nearly closed. Fortunately, there were no piranhas in the pool.

And then when the local rock and roll group took limousines to hidden spots in Joshua Tree and sat drinking Tequila Sunrises at dawn posing for their album cover blasted on peyote, I shrugged. That week in Taos had been quite enough of ethnic purity for me. I hated turquoise and cactus and leathery-skinned Indians wrapped in pastel flannel plaid blankets from J. C. Penney's. Let people from New York and Detroit adore Indians and load themselves with squash blossoms and weaving and be what Alec Guinness, as Prince

Faisal, accused O'Toole of being in *Lawrence of Arabia* when Guinness narrows his eyes and assumes a grave and ironic attitude: "I fear you are a desert-loving Englishman, Mr. Lawrence. No Arab loves the desert; we love cool trees and green grass. Are you, Mr. Lawrence, a desert-loving Englishman?"

And so the last time I went out to the desert, when I was twenty-one, with my sister and her boyfriend and my boyfriend, we all got stuck in a sand storm and the electric windows of the old '52 Cadillac refused to budge and stayed open. I declared, then and there, that I preferred the ocean and would never be crazy enough to go to the desert again.

The peace that some claim to embrace in the sand has never happened to me, although I've always had hopes that a certain dryness would calm me down. I like hot, searing, bloodless air—so hot that you don't even have to breathe.

The trouble with the idea of a desert island is that, if you really think about it, it's not going to be desert in the middle of the ocean. It's going to be humid like Hawaii and Manila and rain every day. And humid you can get in New York.

For years Nikki Kroenberg had been a sort of *House & Garden* figurine to me. She was the wife of a hip lawyer in San Francisco and while he defended liberal, fashionable (rich) causes, she was always photographed stepping out of a Mercedes wearing understated garments that weren't so understated that they didn't state clearly that she was dutifully willing to rise to the occasion of her birth (she was from an old San Francisco via Boston family) and lend her presence to the opera, the children's charity ball, the opening of a new wing at the museum.

Whenever she considered something like taking courses or redoing the living room, I would always hear about it. People made phone calls at the slightest thing she did. They were helpless. The information about her was either extremely personal, like knowing what color she was doing her New York pied-à-terre bathroom, or mythically fashionable, like captions under photographs that said, "Sitting to the right of the ambassador from Sweden is Mrs. Nikki Reese-Kroenberg of San Francisco."

We all hate Jane Powell. There's nothing worse than a tiny figure cheerily cadenza-ing through the kitchen, sparkling up the dishes, accompanied only by a spunky robin redbreast on the sunny yellow windowsill. On the other hand, what is a size-three person to do? Most of the ones I know get migraines in the back of one eye. Their look of despair and hopelessness gives them weight and dimension. But it's odd to think that they all seem to have arrived as though by magic at migraines over the last decade or so. In earlier years, if you were light as a feather, you'd counter like Barbara Stanwyck with a voice of granite quarries and rainbow invitations. Nowadays, like everything else, people just take the first thing they see and it's migraines one-and-all. But it's better than Jane Powell.

So Nikki Kroenberg, I learned from the start, had migraines. The pain enhanced her wispy little frame and gave her gravity. The pain seemed cruel and undeserved like those ads about starving children in *The New Yorker*.

Her size lent something tragic and theatrical to Nikki that made everyone want to smooth things out for her. People forgave her her bathrooms and photo captions because of her constant agonizing migraines. Even from afar, like I was, I wanted to make her smile. Laughter, of course, would be out of the question, for how could one ever make a fragile, ill little thing like Nikki laugh?

But the truth was she *did* laugh. People always forget to tell you the most important part, and in all those phone calls I never once heard that she'd said something funny or thought something was funny. Nikki, however, was completely at the mercy of low-brow buffoonery, slapstick, and clowning. Nothing pleased her as much as the time a judge fell off his podium, pushing a water pitcher onto the Bible someone was using to take an oath. She squealed with joy, pure hilarious joy. The first time I heard her I knew the *real* reason everyone spent so much time worrying about her headaches.

Saul Kroenberg, the lawyer-husband, kept Nikki's San Francisco mansion filled with criminals or the falsely accused or Panthers' old ladies on their way to China.

Nikki had come to L.A. to decorate the law offices of a friend of her husband's. It was her first "job" and she approached it with terror and seriousness. She took a penthouse suite at the Chateau Marmont (she hated the Beverly Hills and the Beverly Wilshire because they were Too Big). She didn't know whether she liked Los Angeles since she never ventured out in it and got all her food by calling the Chalet Gourmet or Greenblatt's. She never would leave her apartment unless she was pushed from behind. She got a headache at the mere mention of a party. She saw no reason why she shouldn't make you scrambled eggs if you proposed going out to dinner. She had her hair cut very short so she'd hardly ever have to go to the hairdresser. Because she hated the building, she only went to the office she was supposed to decorate once and took the plans home. The only place she ever went by herself was to the doctor.

Sara, a high-powered, devastating, brilliant young woman who was my friend, was one of Saul Kroenberg's junior clerks in his San Francisco office but she was often in L.A., and it was Sara who kept me abreast of Nikki's life. When I first met Sara, she was still at Berkeley. She never for one moment got sidetracked by a cosmetic counter and would just as soon have worn Che's old clothes (she was always in jeans—not French-cut—and beatnik sturdy noisy sandals).

As the years passed and Sara became more and more involved with Nikki, she began to don skirts and sleek St. Tropez T-shirts and subtle blond streaks, and a newfangled English accent. One day she said, "I quite like Nikki, actually."

"Do you actually?" I answered. "How lovely for you."

"Aw, come off it," she said.

"Well, really, Sara, what's to like about her?" I asked. "From your descriptions, all she does is mope."

Sara was the type who'd plow right through moping women. She'd lived on a kibbutz for four years and migraines were not in her repertoire.

"She'll be in L.A. for a while," Sara said. "And I'm going to be busy in Oakland. So why don't you give her a call? She'll need someone like you to boss her around."

That night Sara brought Nikki to a gathering of *au courant* magazine people waiting for the coke guy, who'd promised to be there by 7:30 and had just telephoned to say he'd be there in fifteen minutes, that he was two blocks away but had gotten hung up. We were all nervous; he was an hour late already and I'd never waited for a guy involved in real crime before where thousands of dollars were piled up on the coffee table waiting to change hands. Nikki sat curled in the corner of a large overstuffed chair, motionless. I liked her clothes and how she sat. Most people just under five feet feel called upon to prove their normalcy by sporting giant flower prints and sitting up nice and tall. But Nikki wore a tiny smocked little old-fashioned dress with crochet trimming. In spite of her girlish posture and quaint baby-colored dress she looked oddly ominous. Her skull, her cheekbones, the brutal cut to her mouth all were Egyptian and timeless. Her skin was the tone of the desert, no traces of rose, neutral. And just as you thought she was a complete reptile in doll's clothes, she'd raise her eyes and there was the most wonderful surprise—her eyes were warmly golden near the pupil and became violet at the iris's edge.

We were all nervous about the coke dealer, except for Nikki, who yawned and closed her eyes.

"Doesn't she care?" I asked Sara.

"She doesn't take cocaine," Sara said. (Too high-class to take cocaine, eh? I said to myself. That *is* aristocratic in this day and age.) But she cleared this up right away saying, "I just *can't* take it, it's not that I *won't*! My nose bleeds for two days, I've taken so much."

At the end of the evening when Sara suggested that I call Nikki, I figured maybe it might be O.K.

Nikki and I had several late, hour-long phone conversations in which she explained in great detail the problem of the interior of the law office. A fool had painted the foyer deep tangerine so that now it was very difficult to imagine what color she could use for the various law partners that wouldn't overwhelm and clash. She'd wanted to color the rooms something devastating like peach or royal blue but she knew that the clients would cave in in such surroundings and yet . . . she refused to surrender to cream.

"How about gold and purple like your eyes?" I suggested.

"Gold and purple!" she cried, swept away in peals of joy, the laughter of a small boy helpless in the face of the ridiculous. She even dropped the phone.

I was hers forever.

The next day she invited me over for coffee at eleven in the morning and when lunchtime rolled around, I decided to try to persuade her to come to Ports with me, although I knew it was probably impossible. I wanted them to see her, those eyes and that entire accomplishment of an immaculate conception of understated power. Of course, Nikki was not an actress; that was the whole point. She was real.

But she wanted to make me some chicken; she didn't want to go out. It was too hot or too cold, would I like a drink instead, a joint? What was the restaurant called again? She'd never heard of it, but she didn't like restaurants, she never liked them, she hated them. It would probably be too crowded, too empty, too late. At last I backed her out the door and into the Chateau elevator and told her that if she hated it too much, I'd bring her straight home.

"What I really hate about going places like this," she said, balking when we got to my car, "is that everywhere I go I see people I've met before with Saul and they never remember me, even after we've met five times."

"*I* remembered you," I reminded her. "I thought you were quite memorable."

"The first time we met was three years ago at Jack Tribune's brunch in San Francisco. Then we met one night at Perry's. And another time at a screening at Francis's. And once at Sara's."

"That's only four," I said. "And what can you expect for being so little?"

I kind of pushed her into the car and drove off quickly to Ports.

We sat in a dark table in a dark corner. The knife by Nikki's place was dirty. I could have killed them, I really could have. Why did *her* knife have to be dirty the first time she came to Ports? Get a grip on yourself, I said to myself, and took a 10 mg. Valium. I got an even-tempered, smiling grip on myself, which was the least I could do, because Nikki, I could see, was nervous enough for two full-grown people. She leaned forward to me and said, "Don't look now but that man in back of you is one of my husband's clients. He's trying to remember where he met me. He lived in our house for a week."

The man got to his feet, looked puzzled as he put down his tip, and finally left Ports with his lunch companion, a slight edge of bemusement around his shoulders.

"That's why I hate going anywhere," she scowled. "I only like places like coffee shops where no one like that would go."

She was beginning to relax and she told me her plans for the weekend. It was Friday, so the following morning her friend Janet would drive her to Palm Springs, where one of her husband's partners had offered her the use of his house.

"Oh, and I *love* it there so much," she said with all her heart. "The architecture looks like nothing at first but then you start to get this feeling...this *security*. Like you'll never have to go anywhere else. Oh, I *love* it."

"I suppose the desert's okay, if you're in a fortress," I said, watching as she took a small bite of salad and then pushed the plate aside, horrified at something about it.

"Why don't you come?" she asked.

I couldn't believe it. A whole weekend with such an exotic in the desert?

"There's nothing to do all day there but sun," she explained/apologized. "But it's very quiet. You might like it. Why *don't* you come!" she warmed to her cause. "We could leave right now."

"But Nikki..." I said. "Really?"

"We could take the Mercedes," she went on, cresting. "Oh, it would be so heavenly just to go right now. Can you drive a stick?"

"I can drive a stick," I said, "but I can't drive on the freeway. It makes my hair white." (Since my return from Bakersfield when I'd almost gotten sucked off the Grapevine in the wake of a giant truck, I'd vowed never to go on the freeway again.)

"You *can't* drive on the freeway?" she asked. "*I* can't either. Especially if another car is around."

"So see," I said, "I wouldn't be able to drive you."

"Oh, but you must come anyway," she said. I guess the surprise and happiness of meeting another human being who couldn't drive on the freeway outweighed my phobic weirdness. "Maybe someone else..."

"Well, we could get Shawn. He's a great driver. But he doesn't get finished with what he's doing till six. You'd really love him. All women do."

"Are you sure?" she asked. "I'd hate to be stuck out there with someone who wasn't..."

I telephoned Shawn. He follows fashion, so naturally he knew who Nikki Reese-Kroenberg was, and what a curiosity (if nothing else) it would be to spend a weekend in the house of Peter Sanrich IV. However, Shawn had committed himself to helping a friend shoot some pictures and wouldn't be free till seven. It was a time when Shawn and I were spending all our weekends together, behaving like lovers, groping under clothes in movies, and slipping into tiled bathrooms at parties. We even went so far as to throw lustful glances at each other across crowded rooms. So you can imagine how tantalized I was by the idea of spending a whole weekend with him lying in the sun and going to bed early. I could picture everything: Shawn would charm Nikki, charm those migraines away, and then we'd have this incredible creature for a friend, and if Shawn and I ever went to San Francisco, we'd get to visit her. And not only that, but Janet, Nikki's friend who would be joining us, had always been a friend of mine; she was extremely easygoing and was always up for a good time. By the time I got through imagining how heavenly it was going to be, the idea of *not* going made me weak. Panicky. Especially when, after I came back from talking to Shawn, Nikki said, "I don't know... I think I might be getting a headache. Maybe we should forget it. Maybe I should just go home and lie down."

"Really?" I said, trying to keep the panic from my voice and thinking quickly. "I think it'll be better driving out after the sun sets. Not so hot. Hardly any cars. And besides, I know you'll just love Shawn." And then I remembered to add, "He's color-blind."

"Color-blind?" she said. She was instantly captivated. I knew she would be. Shawn's being color-blind was one of the things that had hooked me in the first place. It was so ... otherworldly. He could not tell the black-and-white TV apart from the color set—it wasn't just greens and reds as with most color-blind people. "Gee ..." Nikki said, "I wonder what that's like. Ohhh, I'd love to meet him."

"We'll go to your apartment and then mine and pack," I said, rolling her out of Ports on the momentum of Shawn's color-blindness. Nikki, like me, was a slave to color and thought about it over and over. For someone to be without that sense would amaze her, fascinate her. And already I could see her looking out at Santa Monica with new eyes.

And to sort of deflect any second thoughts Nikki might have, after I'd loaded up the car with our stuff and it was still too early to go to Shawn's, I suggested that we visit my friend David, who had, just that day, been released from the hospital. Nothing like a sick friend, I always say, to counter a tendency toward migraine. I was pretty certain that Nikki was one of those people who liked discussing hospitals, operations, doctors, and specialists. David would be just the thing to keep her amused until we could get to Shawn's color-blindness.

(If you're wondering why I was tossing my friends at Nikki like fish, you're probably a person who has no tendency for society and who does not like to spend hours on the phone reliving parties. You do not like to find things out from women. One afternoon I was sitting on a veranda at a party with about six women and the information that was exchanged, commonly called gossip, was enough to run the world for months. Suddenly a hush fell over the women and I looked around and there was a man. The women slid masks over their faces, the subject changed, the man said, "What are all you girls doing out here? Come in and join the party." And the summit conference was over. Nikki was a masterpiece of this classic form; she understood everything about clumsily arranged dinner parties, about divorce and hospitals and who sat where. And if you're still wondering, I was more fascinated with her than Palm Springs, Barbados, and Paris combined. She was very rare.)

I also told Nikki that David was in the throes of being separated from his wife, who had quietly "suffered" for ten years while she got her doctorate in anthropology. Now that she was finished, she had decided that the whole marriage had been wrong from the start. There'd been some sort of altercation in the hospital parking lot that day, when she'd come to pick David up to take him to his new, empty, bachelor flat. She'd actually thrown a tire iron at him, she was so pissed off at having spent all those dreary years with such a male chauvinist pig.

"So David," I finished, "is not going to be in the most robust condition."

David was immediately soothed by Nikki's adept handling of people just out of the hospital. She had just the right passive quality, unlike me, who went pacing all around looking for a flat mirror and a razor blade.

I went into the bathroom and did as much cocaine as I possibly could, and when I came out, Nikki was inviting David to come along to Palm Springs the next day; Janet would pick him up. "It'll be good for you to get away," she said, kindly. "And there's nothing to do there but lie in the sun."

"Gee, that sounds nice," David said. She was being so pretty, just looking at her made him feel better. "I'd really like to come. I've never been to Palm Springs."

"David's never really been anywhere but New York," I explained, "even if he's been living in L.A. for twelve years."

David is one of those steadfast New York City comedy writers. He wrote comedy every day—I could never quite imagine how one writes comedy, but you get paid $2,000 a week for those TV shows, huge clumps for pilots, and at least $150,000 for a screenplay, if your agent is any agent at all.

David had never become a Californian (for which I was grateful—he never did those damn double-knit jump suits or those damn gold chains or those Gucci shoes or any of the rest of those things New Yorkers do when they become Californians). David never learned to sail, never bought a Porsche or a Mercedes, and never talked about movies in terms of how much money they made. The only thing David does that *is* Californian is not eat meat.

Poor David limped on his crutches and waved at us from his bachelor-flat doorway as we left.

"That was awfully nice of you to invite him," I said to Nikki. It was.

"Well," she said, lowering her eyes, "he looked like he could use some sun."

What an odd woman, I thought to myself, driving us over to Shawn's. She really does hate parties and crowds and she really does love people one by one in such a way that she's bound to always be involved in parties and crowds. She can't truly believe all that paranoia about people not remembering or liking her. She couldn't, I thought, really *believe* that junk.

The trouble was that Shawn is not only color-blind, he also has no sense of things like hours, days, or the pain that certain of us have when dealing with waiting. My sister said, "If you want to keep Shawn, you're going to have to carry a book." That way, all those leisurely situations where Shawn would go to pick up his dry cleaning and leave me in the car and get into a half-an-hour discussion with the old lady who was always so happy to see him and have a nice chat about the neighborhood . . . that way, I could just read my Virginia Woolf. But when we got to Shawn's, I had Nikki with me, so I couldn't very well read (although, by god, I'd bought a dandy new yellow book called *Granite and Rainbow*, and since I'd already re-read *The Common Reader* over and over, you can imagine how the promise of this new bunch of essays lurked in my brain).

There are a lot of people who don't grow limp with hatred when they're kept waiting. I know a whole bunch of people who don't consider the concept of fifteen minutes time at all. So if they say they'll meet you at 11:00 and they show up at 11:25, they apologize (if they remember) for being ten minutes late—the other fifteen minutes never existed and there is some sort of common understanding among most people that those fifteen minutes are a grace period. Since I've started carrying a book everywhere, even to something like the Academy Awards, I've had a much easier time of it, and the bitterness that shortens your life has been headed off at the pass by the wonderful Paperback. Light, fitting easily into most purses, the humble paperback has saved a lot of relationships for me that would have ended in bloodshed.

(My sister is now working on the question "How do you love someone and not take them personally; not care?" I told her that when she figured out the answer to tell me, and I promised not to tell anyone.)

Shawn and the photographer had only just begun to get the lights set up. Shawn was modeling for a Scotch ad. He was supposed to sit in front of a dignified polished desk that looked like it inhabited an English country house library rather than Western Avenue with its incredible varieties of sexual bargaining going on right outside below his window. Poor Nikki had to step through this bazaar of mostly high-heeled young men to reach the foot of Shawn's stairs. Shawn's apartment itself was off a little blameless courtyard surrounding a forty-year-old rubber tree; he lived at the top of some steps on the second floor and looked out over all the traffic on Western. He had draped his windows in dark crimson velvet (which he thinks is blue) and turned the medium-size front room into an English library out of *Lady Windermere's Fan*.

"Is he drunk?" Nikki asked right off, taking one look at the Scotch.

At least, that's what I figured she assumed from, but I thought it was inauspicious of Shawn not to even have the lights set up. It takes two hours to set up the lights and fifteen minutes to take the pictures, and meanwhile Nikki thought he was drunk.

"They just have to finish setting up the lights," I told Nikki, trying to make it sound simple. "Why don't we wait in the kitchen and I'll make us some tea?"

And so, from the kitchen, I could hear them setting up and set-ting up the lights. It was really a trick, too, because there was a mir-ror in back of Shawn that had to reflect Shawn but not the lights or the camera. I could imagine it taking all night. And there was my lovely Virginia Woolf, virgin, in my purse, but how could I for one moment let Nikki's attention wander off by itself where it might get a headache? It got to be about 9:30. I had taken two more Valiums (unbeknownst to anyone) and snuck about a quarter of a bottle of straight rum into my mouth when no one was looking.

"I don't know," Nikki said finally, putting down her *Rolling Stone* and looking as though she were suddenly wondering how she'd wound up in this strange kitchen with these strange people on this abominable street on some obvious misadventure, when all she'd wanted was to lie in the sun by herself in a fortress alone with some proper humans who knew what they meant when they said 7:00 p.m. "I feel so tired," Nikki said, "I think I'll just stay back at the Chateau tonight and leave tomorrow with Janet."

"I suppose you're right," I said, finally beaten. I would kill Shawn, I would stretch it out over the next thirty years so that he would have decades of nasty remarks hurled at him if he happened to run into me anywhere. I would tell everyone I knew what a LATE bastard he was and I would be so clever about it that the idea of being late would suddenly become the eighth deadly sin; it would be worse than glut-tony or sloth—lateness. The fact that he was doing us a favor driving us out there had long ago sunk out of sight.

"Look," I said, "you want to just wait five more minutes and then we'll go? At nine thirty-five we'll leave. What's another five min-utes?"

"Well…" Nikki said. Even she could not object to five minutes because, unlike me, she belonged to the great mass of people who discount minutes.

She agreed. I was on my way back to the kitchen when I bumped into Shawn. "Well"—he smiled—"we're all finished, darling."

It was 9:34 and 59 seconds.

Nikki insisted on sitting in the back seat, huddled and drawn in upon herself as though trying to be brave and disassociated. Shawn was completely unaware of my wrath or Nikki's sadness. The two hours we'd spent in his kitchen waiting, if they crossed his mind at all (which I doubt), were simply a minor inconvenience.

We slid out onto the freeway, which was fairly empty, and I tried to relax and to forget that only moments before I'd been resigned to not going.

Since neither Shawn nor Nikki had eaten all day, they both were hungry and they discovered right away a mutual ability to eat trash. I know that Shawn subsists on white sugar and white flour, and I try not to remind myself that that's what his body is made out of. And Nikki likes trash because no one could possibly recognize her in those places. Having trash in common, they agreed to stop at the first likely-looking crime-against-nature we passed. I told them the Steve Martin story about how there's a big vat in the back of those places that contains various textures but everything is made of the same basic substance: the "hamburger," the bun, the milk shake— all are the same stuff from the same vat but each is squeezed from different faucets, even the cardboard box.

We pulled in to a place called Tandy's. Tandy's had been created out of a gutted supermarket, so that nothing they did would ever make it seem cozy or human; the scale was all wrong for mankind— like a train station. I ordered tea even though I know that the dye they put in restaurant tea seems poisonous.

Nikki ordered the fish plate and french fries and Shawn ordered a grilled cheeseburger, and "lots of ketchup" they both told the waitress.

I sat there watching them carry pale french fries to their mouths and actually eat them. The bleak drear light overhead that remained from the supermarket threw hideous Diane Arbus fatality onto the only other people in the restaurant. Three young men who sat at the counter and were so stumped and ill-nourished that they didn't even have enough élan to appreciate our waitress, who was only nineteen and not yet turned to cardboard.

The only art at all on the wall was by the door, where a large poster in color described the interesting possibilities of joining the Marines and an attached cardboard dispenser gave out free brochures printed in four colors on both sides. The printing must have cost a fortune considering the quality of the paper.

Nikki and Shawn did not leave Tandy's with the calm happiness of the well fed, I'll say that for them at least. They were heading back to the car with enough decency to look betrayed.

"How can you eat that stuff?" I asked Shawn when we were again on the highway and Nikki was sitting in back with her arms folded across her birdlike chest.

"Mark always used to be mad at me for that," Shawn said. "I always hated it that he cared so much about food. Food for me is just something you eat and then forget about. Except that place . . . Tandy's."

So that's how they do it, then. I'd always wondered.

Forty-five minutes later, Nikki directed us to turn right to a hilly road and we drove in silence for a while, in the empty desert, until we were there. The million-dollar house.

Before us was a high white wall that enclosed, I figured out later, the entire rectangle of the building, a rectangle that sort of slanted down a sloping hill—a rectangle that was perhaps ninety feet deep and forty feet across. The wall was as high as two men, and it was painted that glaring North African white you see in pictures of Tunis, where everything has to be white to reflect away the sun. In the middle of the white wall were two large doors. Outside the wall, the car was perfectly safe in the empty desert. The left door was a large glass panel that slid open when Nikki put a key in an invisible lock. She reached for a light which suddenly lit all of it as we descended, enclosed by high white walls, down, down, down to the pools. Two pools, one cool and large and one small and hot with a Jacuzzi. Nikki slid the glass shut behind us. The air was hot and quiet.

As soon as Nikki had locked the door, the world—all of it and its cheeseburgers and waits and colors—all of it disintegrated into a stark, bone white.

Nikki's face smoothed out into the spell of utter moonbeams; Shawn unbuttoned his shirt and let it billow out behind him in air I hadn't known was moving; and I, in this strange blank space, felt like I'd come someplace where the command was to clear one's brain and be carried along in an undertow of austere pleasures of the flesh. This would not be a place to even eat; it was a place for the body to rest.

"The only trouble with this place," Nikki said as we stood there, "is it will drive you completely crazy in three days. Sometimes less."

We were only staying for two, but I felt at that moment that if I'd had my typewriter and some paper I could have written a novel so white that people would have kept it beside them always to empty their minds. I wish she hadn't said that about going crazy just when we'd come in.

The place had a way about it that made you gravitate toward the pools and generally toward the left. There was a square structure divided into four guest quarters. Each unit was fit for a king, or a child—it was a perfect human dwelling with no extras, all plain surfaces and simple, rather hard beds (that were made by invisible servants in the morning while we were out by the pool). It was like in Cocteau's *Beauty and the Beast* when she comes into the palace and even the chandeliers move when she does. The minute you stepped into one of the guesthouses, you knew all there was to know about it and you knew that there was nothing missing... Everything slid, the doors, the drapes, the glass shower partition, the drawers and windows, everything.

Shawn and I put our hastily-gathered-in-L.A. things down on a dressing table place and went to join Nikki in the main room.

Nikki too had brought something to look at. An Italian *Vogue*, one of those issues with the entire fall collection for cold European winters delineated in gorgeous color, the issues that cost five dollars. On the cover was a furry-hooded Susan Blakely model, with skis just barely visible leaning against her shoulder. Her eyes were winter blue.

"I hate the cold," Nikki said.

"How can you stand San Francisco?" I said. "It's freezing there."

"It *is* freezing," she said. "Maybe I'll divorce Saul and move to the desert. Only..." She sighed and turned pages of the *Vogue*.

"Only what?" I asked, pouring myself a glassful of tequila.

"Only he wouldn't care. Once we talked about divorce and he said that if we *did* get one, he'd naturally keep the house since he needed it for business. I *made* that house." She looked out at the pools where Shawn was already being a dolphin. "He doesn't know how hard that house was to get running. Now *this* house is wonderful. You hardly even need servants."

"It'd be a great place to start a nunnery," I said.

The living room, the main room, was a rectangle that ran crosswise along the side of the hill counter to the pull of gravity. It had ceilings that were twelve feet high, as high as the walls around the place, and the walls of the rooms looked like the same white brick. The walls facing the pool and the walls facing the guesthouse were all glass sliders. It was the kind of glass that made you put your hand before your face each time you went in or out, to make sure you didn't bash your nose (which I did the first night because of the tequila).

Nikki was picking over the records and had put on a stack of trash—throwaway music. Music is painful to me in the best of times. I decided to drink half a bottle of tequila and go back to the guesthouse and read what Virginia Woolf had to say about "The Narrow Bridge of Art" in her first chapter.

Not that I like to blame things on tequila, but it must have been something like that because I began sobbing and poor Shawn found me that way. I accused him of trying to fuck Nikki, which came to me in a flash as a likely and much easier story than how the Stones were dropping their beer-can music all over the pure, Georgia O'Keeffe landscape.

"You'll see," he said, cheerfully, "tomorrow it'll be a beautiful day and you'll have a *dread*ful hangover. Which you deserve."

At 7:00 a.m. I awoke with a throbbing headache, a dry mouth, and Shawn pointing to me saying, "You said the worst things last night. You were just absolutely bonkers. And I hope you have a hangover."

"Oh..." I said, hanging over the side of my bed.

"Oh, look," he said, springing into the bathroom with boundless Robin Hood leaps. "Alka-Seltzer."

"Oh..." I said, trying not to hang over so far I'd fall off completely.

"How do you manage to look so fresh when you're so nasty inside?" he asked, bringing me the Alka-Seltzer, and pushing my hair out of it so I could drink it in its pure state.

"Because..." I said, "*I* at least don't smoke."

(It's the only thing I don't do, smoke. It's what saves me. In the mornings. I just remember that Nikki and Shawn both smoke and a natural sense of superiority rises from beneath the slime. It's true.)

We'd come on Friday night so it was Saturday morning when I awoke painted into a corner with nothing but Alka-Seltzer to narrowly bridge me out to the pools. There were two windows, large rectangular holes in the walls with vertical bars on them. The windows were high up in the walls so that I could rest my chin on the sill. There was no glass in these windows, nothing slid, there were just bars. I stood for a long, long time looking out the window at the pastel empty desert in the distance and the rabbits and lizards and funny-looking other things in the foreground and I realized that the bars were not to keep us in or the masses out (for what masses would come all the way out to this empty hold-up?); the bars were to keep the tumbleweeds out of the pools. Shawn came up behind me and rested his chin on my shoulder and his palms on either side of me on the sill and it was absolutely silent and perfect, and I was beginning to feel the way you must on a long ocean voyage with Melvillean empty spaces. It was a chance for me to think and think except Nikki put "Blood on the Tracks" on and slid open the glass to announce her tiny presence. I wished she'd have migraines in perpetuity.

"I have a terrible hangover," I decided to explain, wincing. "Could we...?"

"Oh... sure," she said, and turned it down. She didn't even care, it was just something you did, like set the table, music.

The day was as though we were on a highway going ninety miles an hour toward an enormous mountain—noon—which we thought must surely come closer any moment, but by 9:30 it was still the same size, just as far away. By 10:45 it was still no nearer, time simply did not pass. Janet had telephoned Nikki early and said she would be leaving by 9:00, so we expected that they'd show up at the latest by 11:00. But after months, 11:00 came, and they did not. There was to be a noon, but we had learned from the morning that it was going to happen somewhere in the distant future, and meanwhile we actually began to laugh at how the time had so easily snapped our lives like old sticks. I loved hearing Nikki laugh; I'd forgotten.

By 11:30, David and Janet were still not there. "Maybe," I suggested, "they fell in love and decided to stop at one of those closed-circuit-movie/water-bed places and his crutch poked a hole in the bed and they both drowned. Maybe they had an accident."

"Don't say things like that." Nikki stopped laughing. She was looking like a little scarab, her body oiled for the sun and a big towel around her head. She and Shawn gossiped about people they'd known who died in accidents. I knew no one like that. All my friends died on purpose.

At 3:30 the sun went behind a mountain. The pools were no longer the draw. We'd eaten nothing all day, by the way, but coffee and diet cola. Nothing. I wasn't hungry; it was too light and hot, but Shawn is always hungry and his stomach was doing things, noises. Janet and David seemed part of the missing landscape, they had not even called, and anyway it didn't matter because there was no sun on the pools.

At 4:00 they appeared. David, from the moment he entered the house in his New York clothes and his abysmally unhappy-husband crisis of the separation (she had not telephoned to apologize about throwing the tire iron at him—in fact she hadn't even called to find out if he was all right), should never, ever have come.

Just moments before, Nikki had forgotten and put the record player on its usual too-loud level so that the elegantly talented Leon Russell was Ray Charlesing out into the landscape and living room.

"What is that crap?" David asked when we'd hurried through an invisible sliding door out by the pool to a spot where there was real dirt and true life.

"Rock and roll," I explained.

"I think I'm going to take a cab home," he said.

He was right. He should have got into a cab and bribed the guy to drive him back to L.A. right that very moment. However, I dissuaded him.

Looking back on it now, I wonder if I didn't insist that he stay the same way I tell people how wonderful certain movies were that have nearly annihilated me with their length and breadth. It's as though I want them to go through the same ghastly experience I did just so they won't be let off scot-free. But insisting David stay for a whole day of what I'd experienced with those hours and minutes and noon and all—when he was obviously on the verge of temporary insanity—was really, really carrying coals to Newcastle, spite-wise. To say nothing of my nose, my very own nose—it was as though I'd told someone how great the movie was, and to prove my sincerity I'd even offered to go with them, to spite my face. Perhaps the sun had driven me crazy.

And so the next morning dawned. It dawned hopefully, as though it had total amnesia about the evening before when Nikki and Shawn and Janet had joyfully decided that what we should have for dinner was Hamburger Hamlet food. David, used to the mastered art of French cooking and very special restaurants serving traditional food that had never once passed through Atlanta, Georgia (that's where most of the stuff is frozen, Atlanta, Georgia), was downright horrified and fell into a slough of despond from which nothing would drag him.

The Hamburger Hamlets in West Hollywood and Beverly Hills are fairly decent, for Hamburger Hamlets. The one in Palm Springs is a travesty, and not worth the cardboard the menu is printed on. At Tandy's, the night before, the food had been hot—a quality I'd forgotten could be missing, with everything else that was wrong with it. The french fries at the Palm Springs Hamburger Hamlet were still frozen.

As I say, the sun rose on Sunday letting bygones be bye-frozen-gones.

I woke to find Shawn already out.

He suspected, I suspect, that I was basically in league with David even though David had acted like a total pig the night before, limping like Captain Ahab on his crutches down the nonetheless beautiful twilighted main street of Palm Springs, muttering, "I hate the fucking place. I *hate* it."

By that time, everyone was trying to talk him out of leaving. Probably for the same reason I had, although perhaps Nikki and Shawn really did think a nice day out in that interminable sunshine would be just dandy for someone like David, who was already indignant because of the simple, capitalist security that a place like Palm Springs was a metaphor for. All the black people and Mexicans were in Indio eating decently. Palm Springs was the equivalent of Gucci shoes, and deep down, probably because of my father's similar attitude about the place, I was on David's side.

Shawn, however, had no such ingrown hereditary prejudices and was having a wonderful time looking at rich people and their shops.

I dressed quickly and passed through the sliding thicket, my hands like a blind person's checking the glass, and found Shawn by himself in the kitchen, drinking freeze-dried coffee (the only kind he can make) and looking glum. It was then that he confessed that he longed for doorknobs. "And besides, look at that..." he nodded over at David, who, I saw now, at 8:00 a.m. was hunched over a table with his crutches, talking on a white phone. I could overhear yet another conversation he was having with some long-distance friend about the tire iron in the garage and about "How could she do that to me?"

"Oh god..." Shawn said. "I wish he'd just shut up."

It was the only time I ever saw Shawn be bored by suffering. Usually he would dry lepers' feet with his hair; I've often feared that he'd eventually leave me not for some prettier or richer person, but to perform some Christian act of atonement, like characters named Sebastian in English novels who were always terrific at Oxford, throwing the most romantic caution to the winds and winding up as orderlies in Catholic Beirut hospitals.

Later that day I watched Shawn swim and wanted him to kiss me, and when I asked him, he kissed my foot. I wished I were dead. I didn't like our kisses to be jokes and I was miserable being on David's side but *had* to be there. I would have felt like a traitor to my father if I had indulged in all the pleasures of what I knew to be wrung from the sweat of underpaid workers. The masses.

"Can we leave early?" I asked Shawn in the kitchen that morning.

"No," he said. "Not me. I like it here. I never get to lie in the sun and it's what I like to do best."

At nine, Janet came out, having turned the record player on. We ganged up on her and made her turn it off, and it didn't come back on until Nikki, at ten, absentmindedly put Jimmy Cliff out into the air on her way to the kitchen.

She must, I thought, really, really hate me. Here I've brought this David who's grumbling all night and all day about everything, casting a pall, limping around, reminding us that the outside world is out there and we are not safe, even here, in this place. For even as the hours had plowed us under on Saturday, we were still in a glorious limbo. But now Nikki's hoped-for peaceful weekend had been mangled by David's everything... I mean, I could handle the rock and roll and junk food by myself, but to do it in front of a man like my father was too hard. So there we both were, me and David, hating her music and her choice of restaurants and ruining her weekend.

Janet was marvelously immune to everything. She was completely happy to be out in the sun; she never noticed David for one second except to tell me later, "I knew when I saw him with his briefcase and those clothes that he wasn't in any mood for the desert." (Car trouble had made them late.)

So when Nikki slid the door open and came out to the pools, I was not surprised when she pulled her couch as far away from us as she possibly could and stayed there all day and only talked to Shawn who got her to play gin rummy with him. A miracle, I thought.

Virginia Woolf can't be right. Nothing can come of this insane social impasse. I wanted to write a story about Palm Springs that was going to be sexy. I wanted a story with peace in it, for god's sake. Now I was stuck with this broken romance: Shawn kissing my foot instead of my mouth.

Once, during the day, I tried with my last ounce of energy to cheer things up. I took a shower, combed all my hair back up into a severe topknot (which Nikki had wondered why I didn't do, as she hypnotically reshifted the Italian *Vogue*'s wintery pages—it would, she said, give me a "whole new look"). So I pushed my fluffy bangs off my forehead, my gigantic, immense genetic legacy, father's forehead, that I only ever air when I'm writing and can't stand hair on my face. (When I was nineteen and in a market with my sister who was sixteen, I was wearing my forehead out and a man asked if my sister was my daughter.) Shawn was always pleading with me to look classical and show my forehead, so I thought, Maybe something frivolous and daffy like putting make-up on and wearing earrings and a freshly laundered cotton thing—maybe that'll make everyone better.

I spent a lot of time, smoothing on light-turquoise eye shadow and dark purple mascara. I smelled of Le De Givenchy. My lipstick was three different colors (even though Shawn would never appreciate it). I became more and more happy myself. I looked like an Italian countess. A knockout.

I felt as though I were floating as I left our guesthouse and padded along the white cement to the main room. I made sure I didn't crash into the sliding door and saw Shawn and Nikki and Janet all out by the pools, and I anticipated, by that time almost with joy, what an apparition I'd be. What a break in the monotony.

David, I saw, was sitting on the couch balefully reading the L.A. Sunday *Times*. He looked up for a moment as I passed, and said, "What time are we leaving?"

He hadn't even . . . I sailed on past, perfumed to the gills, secure and diaphanous, and murmured in a light, forgiving voice, "Shut up."

David went right over the edge. It was all he needed. A joke.

"Don't you ever tell me to shut up!" he snarled. "Just don't you *ever* tell *me* to shut up. How dare you tell me to shut up!"

"I'm sorry," I said. "I apologize. I don't know when we're leaving. I wish I were dead."

I came out, then, to the pools, shaken—and not only that, but I'd actually forgotten how I was looking.

"Ooooooooo," Nikki said, "how pretty! Oh, it looks so pretty. Oh, you *should* wear your hair that way. It's so ... I don't know. Pretty."

Janet and Shawn too were nice but I thought that of all the days in my life that were rotten, this one in Palm Springs was probably going to be the worst. In a frivolous kind of way, of course.

At 3:30 the sun went behind the mountain and Shawn agreed finally we could go. I was *so* packed. I'd been packed since 11:00. I'd even packed Shawn. I'd put all our packed things right next to the main entry. My one remaining hope was sitting next to Shawn on the ride home. David would sit in the back seat with his grumbles and his leg, which I hoped would fall off from gangrene, and I would be able to be alone more or less with Shawn in the front and he'd make light of the weekend and save me. So I kissed Nikki (who didn't recoil, an extreme act of self-control, I thought) and Janet good-bye—they were going home together later and would probably pounce on our absence with a sigh of relief. Just the sheer absent quality of us would probably fill them with thanks to God. I tried not to rush out to the car.

David was already there. Shawn was making lovely farewells, for which he would always be adored, since social amenities are his raison d'être.

"How do you feel about sitting in the back?" David asked.

"Rotten," I said.

"Well, I'm afraid you're going to have to because this cast won't fit in the back seat."


"It's like one of those horrible *New Yorker* stories from the thirties," said my friend Irene Kamp. On Monday, I decided to telephone Nikki and humbly apologize for spoiling her weekend and wrecking her life. And Nikki was so overjoyed to hear from me, I could *hear* in her voice her surprise and relief that I'd telephoned. She said, "I thought you guys all hated me. That's why I stayed in my room until ten. I thought you were all hating me and saying things about me, how horrible I was."

"You mean," I asked, "you thought we all hated you for inviting us out to lie in a millionaire's sun and had decided not to forgive you?"

"That wasn't how I looked at it," she said. "I just thought you were mad at me for deceiving you about Palm Springs, for making you think you'd like it. See, I really like it, I do. But I see how I tricked you into coming."

"Oh god, Nikki..." I said.

And slowly we began to talk of other things, especially my forehead, which Nikki thought I should always reveal. But I knew I wouldn't.

The peace that some claim to find in all that sand will never happen to me in Palm Springs, no matter how I hope for flat dry hot air so bloodless that I won't even have to breathe or think.

Sometimes when Shawn is very peaceful with pastel rainbows blanketing us, he'll put his hand on my thigh and say softly, "Oh, you know, one day let's go back... Do you think we can? To Palm Springs. I loved it there with you." The hard granite facts have already melted into the story I wanted to tell you about the desert and the hot nights and sexy pools; for Shawn the whiteness of the bones has already become romance.

# EMERALD BAY

THE SKY was bright hot and smogless and the freeway was thinned out from the Friday-night rushers. Cars that drove along with us were filled with the slower people who drive south on Saturday mornings. No matter how many times they tell you that leaving the city makes you feel better, you never believe it because while you're in the city it doesn't seem that bad. But when we'd turned south on the Santa Ana Freeway (I won't let Shawn take the San Diego Freeway because it is too ugly for words or holiday rides, even if you are going to wind up in Laguna at the end more quickly), layers of distraction were swept away like furniture on a stage at the end of a scene. Laguna was to be the next act, the strange little private section called Emerald Bay.

"Emerald Bay..." I had said when Shawn suggested we go. "How unsuperstitious."

"How what?" he laughed.

"You can't go naming places Emerald Bay and expect to get away with it. The gods'll come out of the sea and poison the food."

And what were Shawn and I doing away from our natural avant-garde habitat? Especially Shawn, who in those days, before we started going to Laguna and falling in love, used to go to every single party there was. There he'd be. Smiling. Not that I'd see him *everywhere*, but I'd hear he'd been everywhere. He was the first person to invite. He knew people everywhere and of every description, but he preferred those who were sympathetic to the idea of parties. And had money.

He always looked wonderful at a party, like a Henry James fortune-hunting prince—weak and kind—marrying the heiress from Poughkeepsie and being worth every penny she spent on him if it was only for how well he listened. How he looked in those white pants and blue blazers was extra. Slender and smiling with white teeth and sympathy. Shawn knew everyone's birthday. (It was the only thing about him that was the least bit organized, calling people on their birthdays. People would cry if he forgot.)

I was a difficult, mean bitch, whose cat, it was rumored, bit men. (And whose cat *did*.) I lived on a street in the middle of Hollywood with an abundance of palm trees and my orange sunsets over the jacaranda branches. Shawn's always trying to smooth things over and I'm always trying to rumple them up.

"But how will it end?" he worries, sometimes, about me.

"When we all die!" I explain.

"Oh . . ." he says.

It makes him so mildly frustrated sometimes that he is reduced to saying things like, "It'll be good for your *soul* if you try to get along with your grandmother."

"My *soul*!" I drop my fork and feel tears in my nose. "What do you know about souls. You never feel *anything*!"

He looks around anxiously; people sitting nearby in the restaurant are staring hard at their food as their ears turn red. Perhaps Shawn, in the beginning, looked upon me as a challenge. Maybe he felt that he could show me the path to polite and gentle society.

I was somewhat nicer that Saturday than I'd been in a year. My book had come out, and this had put me out of the reach of a lot of old dumb questions and into the land of new dumb questions. But I wasn't as used to the new dumb questions, so when men I had once thought of as wise daddies now asked me "How do you write?" I did not try and spill red wine on their suede pants, I would just smile and say, "On a typewriter in the mornings when there's nothing else to do."

On April 15, 1976, I read in the *L.A. Times* that Phil Ochs was cremated. (I hadn't even known he was sick.) And it turns out he *hung* himself. In the news story it said he'd complained to a friend that he was depressed and "couldn't write." He'd been complaining for years that he could no longer write. I thought he wrote such beautiful melodies you could swim in them. And now he's done such violence to himself, putting a rope around his neck, *hanging* himself, thirty-five years old. New York City style, black and white. No accident. Taking no chances.

Shawn and I passed the Garden Grove exit and the whole of L.A. seemed to drop away from behind us. Shawn's middle-aged Oldsmobile had all the comforts of home, glove-compartment lights that worked, smooth sailing. The enormous part of Shawn that was formed before he came to the Coast, that Charleston boyhood, made it impossible for him to have a car that wasn't as American as lemonade. His profile was silhouetted against the violent green orange-tree leaves that grew in groves beside the freeway. Citrus trees are so green they seem like mescaline hallucinations, even out in Bakersfield.

The Laguna Canyon Road turnoff came half an hour later, and we slowed down to the hilly old two-lane road, I remembered suddenly, of my adolescence and before. Balboa and Newport Beaches, where other people went, had been too crudely yachty for my father, and we had always stayed instead in some overgrown cottage in Laguna. In spite of what a fake artists' colony it was, Laguna was simply irresistible—pottery shops or no. Dumb art galleries inspired TV writers to suggest Perry Mason scripts about art frauds by the sea. But there were flowery hills and horses and cows, nonetheless, and my father was unable to resist, so he used the perfect excuse— that it was nearby—and to Laguna we went.

One Easter vacation, my father subjected himself to a week of Bill Haley teen-agers so that I could be in the middle of the action. But even the teen-agers who came to Laguna were toned down compared to the rowdy ones who went to Bal. (Balboa was so crammed with kids that the whole island was bumper to bumper with radio-blasting cars.) I was not much good as a teen-ager: On the Palm Springs week I bled from my wisdom tooth the whole time, while on the Laguna Easter I got the flu and slept for four days.

Shawn and I entered Laguna from the back, the way you come to Cannes and other seaside resorts. In Cannes the harbor seems to fall open in front of you, but in Laguna it isn't until you're almost upon it that you see the ocean, which seems, consequently, to be in the middle of downtown. One minute it's traffic and stores, the next it's volleyball and the blue Pacific.

One of my first romantic fantasies was that when I grew up and got to have anything I wanted, I was going to have an adorable male companion who drove a 1930's roadster convertible and we'd motor along the French Riviera or up to Santa Barbara or down to Laguna. I had now grown up and had been able to persuade men to take me to the Russian Tea Room for caviar, to the Plaza for lunch, to the Via Veneto for Campari and sodas, and to the Coronado Hotel for cream of asparagus soup—but I had never been able to get one, not *one*, man to take me for a cozy little weekend by the ocean. I'd long ago dispensed with the roadster convertible or the adorable part. And now, there with Shawn, was a dream come more or less true because he was adorable and you could equate a nice American car like he had with a nice American car like I had in my fantasy.

"I've *always* wanted to do this," I told him. "You're so wonderful." (You can tell Shawn things like that without him vanishing, I'd learned.)

We slowed down so much that it was as if we were swimming under water, the sky was so blue, everything else was October amber, or green. Just like in the movies, he took my suddenly small darling hand in his huge rough one and it was just like love. It was peaceful. I was not used to things being peaceful with a man.

Where the Laguna Canyon Road lets out onto the beach and suddenly the water, we turned north and drove up a few blocks past the Victor Hugo Restaurant, where Shawn and I later took Jo one afternoon for three Margaritas apiece. Past the Victor Hugo, on the right, there was an armed guard inside a guardhouse, controlling an electric entrance bar. Beneath the arch (which said EMERALD BAY) the guard made sure that you didn't get in without a pass or a sticker on your car to prove you lived there. There were, I thought, no surprises from without in Emerald Bay. And to make sure you did nothing untoward once inside they had raised lumps in the asphalt on the winding hilly road so you could only go ten mph. "Speed bumps" Shawn told me they were called, and I laughed at the name.

The houses in Emerald Bay were not ostentatious; they were dreamy little "cottages" which cost no less than $250,000 each but looked modest and bashful. They were like those Mediterranean villas from Hollywood movies, clustered cleanly atop Positano. Everything, all the leaves on the trees and geraniums and ivy, was all as clean as could be. The houses were polished to a fine shine; every repair was made before you could say Jack Robinson. Dead leaves must have been removed from trees before they dried up so that no one would ever have to think about things drying up and falling to the ground in Emerald Bay. No unpleasant notions. I couldn't believe my eyes when I first saw the peach-colored bougainvillea stark against a white holding wall—I thought I'd seen everything—but *peach* colored! So flagrant and wild against the hot sky. Shawn kept on driving up the winding road, slowly, because of the speed bumps.

Jo and Mason Marchese were old friends of Shawn's from Charleston, where Mason had been an executive in an electronics firm. When he retired, two years before, they moved to Laguna because they'd come there thirty years earlier on their honeymoon and vowed to return one day to build their own house. When Shawn looked at people he saw wonderful things about them, and his face would sometimes go into a trance, as though he were in love. If he spoke with someone for longer than fifteen minutes it was usually enough time for him to get indelibly enamored of them, but in those days I didn't quite know that, so I was a little surprised at Shawn's awed tone when he told me, "I know you're going to love Mason. He's the king. Of all he surveys."

"The what?" I asked. From where we were, all that could be surveyed was a small notch between two hills that let out to the sea on a private bay that was as green as emeralds until it turned as blue as lapis lazuli.

Shawn pulled the car into the driveway of the first house I'd seen that was not completely hysterical about being perfect. There were untended wildflowers growing around the mailbox stick, for example. The front door burst open and out came Jo Marchese overjoyed to see Shawn (and suspicious about me). We were pulled inside with loud greetings and loud recriminations for not having gotten there the night before. Jo Marchese was a small Midwestern woman who'd been a sculptor all her life, sticking to her guns in spite of being married to a man who kept being transferred by his company to places like St. Louis and Oklahoma City. And of course, everyone loves Mason—he's like Laguna itself; who could resist?

Mason was smiling and much too handsome in an open, Neapolitan kind of easy way. I always get along with men like Mason because they never ask dumb questions, and anyway, no wonder Shawn was so enchanted by him, he was just gorgeous. He had curly gray hair, a curly gray mustache, and green eyes. He did not resist a tendency toward flowered Hawaiian shirts, and I was grateful because it was nice to see those shirts meet their match. He had a beautiful voice, and an expression, when he was as serious as he could get (which wasn't very), like William Shakespeare's.

Most of the time Mason just looked like the benevolent king of all he surveyed, and later, when I watched people come to him with everything from car to tax problems, it was like watching a fairy godfather dispensing answers and advice with humorous nonchalance. Shawn wanted him to be his father. And Mason, apparently, couldn't think of any reason why not. So I became the mistress-in-law.

("I'm completely happy," he told me when they moved into their new house, which hung over the ocean. "I could not get any happier. I have everything I've ever wanted right here." Instead of discovering that he didn't want everything he'd ever wanted like most people, Mason was completely happy.)

But Jo was Shawn's specialty, his own private friend, and they seemed to thrive on constant warfare, tugs of war, and hours and hours of discussions about the couch. (She has *yet* to get this new couch and they've been poring over ads now for as long as I can remember.)

But that first afternoon all I knew was that they really loved Shawn and they lived in a strange place. They didn't seem like the kind of people who'd seek out such exclusivity; they didn't seem as though they'd mind a few dead leaves.

We were told to go down and swim, that they had to go out for a few hours and would be back in time to get dressed and go down to Beth Nanville's get-together.

"Ohhhh . . ." Shawn said, his face falling slightly. "Do we *have* to?"

Mason looked as though he'd just as soon not go either, but only slyly and only for a moment, because Jo was saying, "Now you know, Shawn, that she's my very best friend. Who would I talk to in this ridiculous place if she weren't here?"

"O.K.," Shawn grumbled, like a small boy. "If we *have* to."

Shawn and I put on our bathing suits and speed-bumped the car a mile or so over more of Emerald Bay's private roads, which went under the Pacific Coast Highway and let out onto a private parking lot by the private beach.

"Gol*ly*," I said, "look at all the white folks."

There were scads of goyim: I was probably the only black-hearted Jewess there amid that abundance of Clairol straight blond hair, gingham bikinis, Peanuts beach towels, and estranged-looking young married couples down to visit the folks in the retirement paradise of Emerald Bay—a place no one could afford until they were too old, except the Marcheses, who were moving just as soon as their new house was finished.

Shawn never knows what to say to this kind of rich people, the children of the dull rich. Their parents, their mothers especially, he gets along with fine, but the children, even the ones his own age, don't get his manners or his soft voice.

We walked to as far away as we could get from them and lay down. Now and then the distant volleyball players' voices carried to where we were, but mostly we were alone and in silence with the ocean. I gave myself up to the situation gradually; we were in Orange

County, so of course anything that was fascinating, a new idea, a breakthrough, was kept outside the gates. No art. It was very relaxing, I thought after a while, to be in a place where there could be no surprises, and very relaxing to be with Shawn, who fell asleep the minute we lay down. I drifted away, watching the water until Shawn finally woke up and sat up beside me, brushing my back free of sand and then keeping his hand there.

"This must be the acme of a certain aspect of Western civilization," I murmured.

"The what?" he asked.

"Never mind," I said. It didn't matter that there was no art or thought; it went with the guard at the archway.

We returned to the Marcheses' in time to dress and join them on their walk a block or so down the hill to the Nanvilles'. Shawn had told me that Beth Nanville didn't like him, that she thought he was a waste of time and never understood why Jo liked him. I'd never heard of someone not liking Shawn before.

The Nanvilles lived in a pine house. Their view of the ocean was spectacular but the clothes that they wore and that everyone who came there but us wore were doggedly ugly and meanly unflattering. But well-made, if you know what I mean. It was enough to make you fall into the blues. We *could* have been in the middle of a movie about Positano with maidens gracing the landscape with thick curls and jasmine and songs—and yet in Emerald Bay the men were allowed one crocodile, a tiny one on their shirts (although Mason went ahead and wore the Hawaiian flowers, since he was king). The women were allowed stripes and prints, but only in colors that washed them out or turned them green. And only in styles that took your mind off breasts and hips and put it on hair-sprayed, short, curled hairdos in which they had just invested twenty dollars and an afternoon making sure they didn't look inviting to the touch.

There were no books in the house and no paintings on the walls. There were photographs of the Nanvilles' children, a boy and a girl. And sculpture.

I came to my wit's end in two minutes and hurried into the

kitchen demanding to do something like make the salad dressing. I tasted a leaf of lettuce and undertook to get that salad dressing made right away. Everything was right there, the oil, the vinegar, and salt and pepper. (Nothing like garlic, though, of course, since there probably isn't any garlic in Orange County outside of the Marcheses' house.) Beth Nanville attempted to discourage me, but I wasn't going back out into that living room until I'd had two drinks, and she simply didn't have what it took to make me pay any attention to her.

She was identical to all the other women in the room, perhaps interchangeable with them, except for Jo. She had the same untouchable hair, the same bright-pink lipstick, the same terrible vague look around her eyes that got more confused when she was told that not only was I Shawn's girlfriend (she knew Shawn was gay, and how could he be with me if he was gay?) but I was also a writer. "A writer?" she said. "How interesting."

She wore dismal colors always, powder blue and mustard, and I put her into my "Empty Lady Hanging On" category, for I am quick to categorize and find it saves mountains of time. I figured out later that in her own private way she had some odd version of loyalty; she bought all of Jo's sculptures (the only art in the house) and, once she met me, bought ten of my books. Even if I was Shawn's girlfriend. I think she was such a snob that she felt that God allowed only things of the highest quality into her life, otherwise they wouldn't be there. Maybe. Actually, I can't imagine her buying ten of my books no matter how I try and figure it. And who, among her friends, did she *give* them to?

Scatter Nanville was Beth's husband. How anyone could be called Scatter was beyond me, but he was, and he had a prep-school voice so I figured it was one of those "Bobo" names. I spent a lot of time on the salad, drank two glasses of white wine, and finally got acclimated enough to take a third glass out to the balcony and watch the sun set.

Shawn was there instantly, saying, "Thank *god*. Where *were* you? Mrs. Scott has told me about her hysterectomy for the last ten minutes!"

"That's what you get for being so nice," I said. "Look…"

The sun was setting like the beginning of the world and it was very peaceful, after all, being there with Shawn. I didn't really mind that everyone was so sadly hideous and Nixony, since it sort of isolated me and Shawn on our own little island. Mason came out, his first drink still full in his glass (he was the only person in Emerald Bay who was not drunk by 7:00 p.m.). He stood beside us, watching the sun set.

"Come here often?" I asked him, quietly lascivious.

"I don't know why she always has these things," he said. "She hates to cook."

"It must be great to have your own speed bumps," I said.

"Our house will be finished in a couple of months," Mason said. "You and Shawn are welcome to come down anytime."

"Don't they know they're living in the middle of *it*!?" I asked Shawn the next night as we were driving back to L.A. "Or is part of what they're paying for the pretense that it's not there? I mean, even kings and queens will enjoy the scenery. But these people just act like it's only O.K. if it's locked up and perfectly polished, and they've got their eyes on how spick-and-span everything has to be rather than on the bay or the sunset."

"I know…" Shawn said. "But I like it anyway."

(See how he is?)

Shawn and I went back to Emerald Bay three more times before the Marcheses moved to their own cliff-hanging marvel that they built themselves south of Laguna, alone and rocky. Now and then the Nanvilles would appear, and every single time I'd have to stick close to Shawn to be able to distinguish Beth from the wall. Because I liked Jo so much by that time and felt I could say anything, I asked her one day after Beth had left what she saw in Beth, her "very best friend."

"Beth and I grew up together," she told me. "We've been friends since we were girls. She was always the most beautiful thing I ever saw."

"Beth?" I asked. I mean, Jo knew what was beautiful—you could tell from her art. But Beth was invisible.

"We walked in the rain together when we were girls," Jo said dreamily. "Nothing will ever replace that."

When Jo and Mason moved to their new house, Shawn and I had already developed an easy habit of being able to be on our way down there in two seconds the minute things got the least bit complicated. Any pressing social engagements found us not home. The ocean crashed beneath our window and drove Shawn wild with desire and everyone else to sleep. You could see Catalina Island *and* San Clemente Island, which was really far away.

Jo grew orchids and primroses; Mason grew basil and squash. Their house was on a rough road, but there was no armed guard, and the leaves fell to the ground when they were dead around there. Whales went south in the spring and everyone was in love with whales. I never was able to see one but I take their word for it that they exist, those whales, though by the time I get the binoculars focused all there is is white water.

Once, when Beth Nanville appeared in the living room and I was in a Shawn-inspired mood, I decided to memorize her face so I'd know her when I saw her the next time. But the more I tried to find something to fasten on to, the blurrier she got.

I didn't know what it meant when Shawn telephoned me one evening to say he had to go down to Laguna to be with Jo because Beth had just committed suicide. A huge overdose of Seconal, no note, a locked door that Jo broke down, and mouth-to-mouth resuscitation that saved her life for nine days, though her brain was dead. She never came to. *I* certainly couldn't have lived the life she was living, so remote and empty and clean.

And the next time Shawn and I went down there, I couldn't at first understand why Jo's eyes were so red, as though she'd been crying. I'd forgotten so completely about Beth.

But when Jo and I were alone in the kitchen she told me, "I knew... For the last six months I just *knew*... She'd gone farther and farther away. I can see her standing there—looking at her body that was getting old in the mirror and deciding it was old and imperfect and that she would kill it. You know, she couldn't stand anything that was old."

I tried to imagine this woman whose face I couldn't remember standing naked in the mirror with the emerald bay behind her.

"She always liked you, you know," Jo went on. "She didn't like many young people but she liked you. Not that she ever got over the salad dressing."

"Oh . . ." I said. I couldn't remember and then did.

"Salad dressing was her speciality. They said she made the best salad dressing in Emerald Bay."

"Oh, no . . ." I said.

"And the trouble was that she'd already made the salad dressing when you came in. It was already *on* the salad."

"Oh god . . ."

I wish, now, that I could remember her face or the sound of her voice. But the only things that I really remember are that she left her children $2,500,000 in her will and when I tasted her lettuce I was sure there was nothing on it.

Now that the Marcheses live south, when we come to where the Laguna Canyon Road hits the sea, we turn south, not north. So we don't even have to pass the unostentatious entrance to Emerald Bay, with its modest gateway, easy to miss. And now that I think of it, I can hardly remember what the place looks like—just that the leaves were very clean, that there were those speed bumps, and that they weren't taking any chances. It was hard to believe that Beth Nanville had once walked in the rain with Jo, but long ago she must have. Chances are what one remembers.

# THE GARDEN OF ALLAH

*I saw Gabrielle the other night out hunting in a bush jacket at some museum opening. I asked her if she remembered about the Coyote's Brain, and she cracked her bubble gum and wondered what I was talking about. She was with Edward Sanford, and when I asked him where his wife was (the next one), he said he thought probably Kenya. Gabrielle probably "disappeared" her, too.*

EVER SINCE the Garden of Allah was torn down and supplanted by a respectable savings and loan institution, the furies and ghosts have made their way across Sunset to the Chateau Marmont. The Garden of Allah was originally the villa of Alla Nazimova, a great silent star, until one night when a fire swept down Laurel Canyon, and she was forced to decide what she wanted to save from her grand house—what, in fact, she wanted at all. And she suddenly knew that the flames could consume all she owned, she would leave for New York at once; there was no point in owning anything in Hollywood, and in this she had a curious premonition or grasp of "place." It's a morality tale of the unimportance of material things, though there are those who will say it's about how awful L.A. is.

In 1926 or '7, when the Chateau Marmont was completed, the Garden had already gained its reputation as a place to court disaster, and perhaps that is why the Chateau's basement parking lot is so impossible. Even sober. It's no mean feat to negotiate, with its gigantic pillars everywhere, so they must have meant for all the boozers and dopers and midnight drivers to pull into the open field across the street which served as the parking lot for the Garden, and for the upright citizens to stay at the Chateau. I always park on the street behind the Marmont, for as Mary once explained, "You never can tell, my dear, what little rascals someone may have dropped on their way out for a spin . . . ["Rascals" were pills.] Very bad for the fenders . . ." And she'd add, "Who knows, when you go into the Chateau, in what condition you'll leave . . . never mind what *day* . . ."

You can't tear down places like the Garden of Allah and just expect them to cease. All that Hollywoodness has to go somewhere. And in the end it took refuge in the Chateau.

It had been a long time since I'd been to the Chateau the day I parked my car on the street in back and went to visit Pamela. Three years. Pamela's apartment was one with a northern view that looked out over the back of Hollywood. In 1916, when Alla Nazimova moved across the street, there was nothing whatsoever to see in those hills except brush that turned green with the rain and inflammable in the dry sun. There had never been, I don't think, much holly in those hills, nor is there any such thing as a Hollywood bush or tree or wood or flower. Maybe the name "Hollywood" sounded cozy under all that sky—English and quaint. But like the savings and loan atop the Garden of Allah, you can't just build over and change names, so now the word "Hollywood" does not sound adorable or cozy. And now those hills are teeming with starburst glitter stucco, and Spanish haciendas and A-frames, and it's all so unpromising it's hard to believe that what really happened really happened— that Errol Flynn and Tyrone Power existed, when all the rest is so rickety.

Pamela has begun to write for an English weekly about "Hollywood." She looks like a Moroccan boy whore. The way her hair curls wildly and darkly around her tiny dark face, her embroidered layers of tinkling vests and blouses, her soft desert slippers are always a shock against her well-bred English voice and her flatly pedestrian sentiments. I keep hoping for something that is evil and brilliant to come out of her boyish mouth, but all she ever says is "Why aren't there any men in this town?" or "How many carbohydrates do you think that has?" She writes about her subjects with an earthbound certainty, only fluttering her heart when she sees Robert Redford up close for the first time or when Daniel Wiley returns a phone call.

"Oh, thank god you're here," she says. "Maybe you can help me with this. I've been sitting and sitting all week, staring out the window."

"I don't think the direction is very inspirational," I answer, watching as she pours boiling water into two cups with tea bags in them. Pamela has been away from England long enough to know that no one really cares about "proper English tea." She never liked England besides, and if the whole place disappeared in a sunset it wouldn't damage her the way it damaged me when they tore down the Garden or when I saw a sign in the Twentieth Century-Fox Commissary a couple of years ago that said, BUS YOUR OWN DISHES.

I sit on the floor across the coffee table from Pamela, who sets down our tea. Neither of us takes sugar, although she looks at it longingly before she raises her large eyes to the hill behind the hotel and says, "Do you, by any chance, happen to know Gabrielle Sanford?"

"Everyone knows Gabrielle..." I say.

"Because well, you see, I'm doing an interview with her and you're from here so maybe you can explain..."

"What?"

"The *attitudes*! You people out here have the strangest damn attitudes."

When they tried to tear down Marshall High School, the neighborhood went into such arms that it is still there. It's that kind of civic-minded neighborhood; it always has been. Even when I went to Marshall ages ago, it seemed to me like one of those schools you'd find in Berkeley where everyone paid attention to local elections and trees. Marshall itself is made of brick, with dignified old Torrey pines and scholarly lawns. It's all so normal and American that they always use Marshall on locations when they need a typical Midwestern high school.

Hollywood High, where I was legally zoned, was rounded, voluptuous, palm-treed, and banana-leaved and sprawled out onto Sunset and Highland, where men with convertibles and green eyes cruised by at three to watch the girls. I was afraid to go there.

I lied about my address and enrolled in Marshall. At least for the first year, I told myself, I can keep out of sight during the bloodcur-dling sorority rushes that maim you permanently. Women I know are always saying that they're glad, after all, that they weren't popu-lar in high school, because all the girls who were are now taking Va-lium and are divorced and stupid. But everyone knows that it would have been much better to have been popular in high school when your blood was clean, and pure lust and kisses lasted forever. Choco-late Cokes in high school are better than caviar on a yacht when you're forty-five. It's common knowledge.

It was the end of my first year at Marshall. I had followed along with a couple of girlfriends to a football game to which everyone was going, although I usually drew the line at football. There was a point beyond which I would not lie to myself, and pretending I liked foot-ball was it. Nevertheless, there I was. A bunch of younger kids from King Junior High were sitting in front of us. Each time something happened with the football, they'd all scream and moan just like everyone else. Except for one girl who refused to participate, no mat-ter what. She sat there for all to see with her mousy hair.

"Oh . . . that's just Gabrielle Rustler," one of my friends told me during a lull. "Guys think she's beautiful but she's really a nothing. I mean, she doesn't even comb her hair!"

She heard. She turned around from three rows down and, as first her profile and then her full face appeared, I felt overwhelmingly that my bovine un-Hollywood future of smoothly counseled majors and electives was about to bite the dust.

Gabrielle's face was rueful and cross, but of course men would think she was beautiful. Her eyes were powder-blue ponds of inno-cence.

She gazed at the girl who had spoken; she was chewing about four cents' worth of bubble gum and a pink bubble began to emerge from her pouty lips, a pink bubble that grew bigger and bigger. By the time it became the same size as her heart-shaped face, I was agonized that it would explode. Then just at the perfect moment, she inhaled and the bubble went back inside her mouth. She turned to the game, leaving us with her tangled mousy hair, and the next day I told the upright authorities that I was moving to Hollywood and gave them my right address.

"I quite like Gabrielle," Pamela said, unconsciously dropping three lumps of forbidden sugar into her tea. "She's quite a dear little thing, really."

"Really?"

"Yes, quite dear."

"Gabrielle?" I made sure.

"I saw Edward Sanford, the ex, you know," Pamela went on. "He's remarried."

"Has he?" I asked. "Oh, yeah. I read about it."

"He was very helpful. Said he would always love Gabrielle of course, even though they were just friends...Do you believe they could be just friends? People say he got married on the rebound."

"Do people still say 'rebound'?" I asked.

"But, well, I couldn't help feeling he was really still in love with Gabrielle. Do you think he is?"

"Pamela," I said, "with those people, who *knows* what love is? Is he still living in the house?"

The house and the land on which it stood were both vast. To the left of the house was an unpaved baseball-size field where my car was being parked by a red-jacketed Oriental. It was during the 1967 Monterey Pop Festival, a time when there was a definite place to be, and if you weren't there...well, you were off the bus. The party was given to celebrate Midsummer Night: That night the Sanfords' was the place.

Edward Sanford's family always referred to Gabrielle as "the accident," in sentences that went, "Before the accident we all used to..." Sanford came from one of those old, unsquandered Hollywood fortunes, the origin of which had been named Sanovitch but they changed it. Enough time had passed however to turn them into Sanfords. And Sanfords did not marry Rustlers.

It was not fair of the Sanfords to blame Gabrielle for all of Edward's flamboyant behavior, because even before "the accident" he'd taken to the Sunset Strip with total abandon. And who wasn't fascinated by rock and roll, drugs, and those strange young girls the Mamas and the Papas sang about? We used to see him before he met Gabrielle. He was divinely beautiful with those wide brown eyes and Dionysian attitudes, but he wouldn't give any of the wild girls a tumble, and in those days I used to understand it when he said, "I am not in love." He was twenty-five and had just inherited so much money that he could have financed four movies and had them all be flops. Locally, deep down all that still mattered was movies.

Gabrielle was twenty and entertaining ambitions of becoming a star. She had appeared in several small parts. She couldn't act. She wouldn't have needed to if her cross, frowning personality had translated onto the silver screen. The trouble was that the men who cast her thought she was beautiful, so they put her into wistful, dreamy dresses when they should have handed her a whip and got out of the way.

Edward met Gabrielle one night and they eloped the next.

He put the house in her name as a wedding present and they had been there a couple of years by the time Mary (who seemed to be having the party even though it was Gabrielle's house) asked me to "Come early so we can chat." So there I was, Midsummer Night, early. There was an armed Pinkerton at the door with a guest list and a flashlight.

The living room was sunken and grandiose; there were a shoulder-high fireplace, French windows that opened out to the terrace. Clusters of furniture were here and there. Hung over the fireplace was a big, bad oil painting of a beautiful señorita leaning against a mission archway. The guests were sparsely distributed in small bunches. Gabrielle was sitting hunched over and immersed in a conversation with Marlon Brando.

"My dear!" Mary said, floating like a lilac toward me with outstretched slender arms. Her blond light "bad" hair ("bad" hair in those days was hair that wasn't coarse) defied gravity and seemed to accompany her like a funny angora animal. She was dressed in flowing, translucent lilac cotton with peach slippers; everything floated when she moved. She smelled like lilacs. She had lilac mascara around her eyes and lilac eye shadow that faded into her temples. Her lips were peach. Altogether she looked like a sunrise in paradise.

Nothing held that night together for me but Mary.

Mary knew everybody, which is why she knew me. She was a Sanford, one of Edward's cousins by marriage. Like Edward, she refused to go straight, but she maintained family ties and never flaunted her bohemian sins.

"Let me show you the house," Mary said, and she took me out to the gardens and showed me the peacocks and the fountains and told me that she'd come to the house when she was little and it had belonged to an English actor who had large Easter parties. We smoked a joint and stayed out too long.

When we returned I saw Gabrielle give Marlon Brando a perfunctory smile, disclosing her perfect little arching gums over her perfect white L.A. teeth. She moved swiftly across the living room and stopped in front of us.

"Hiya," she said to me and to Mary. "Where've you been?"

"Have you met? . . ." Mary introduced us.

"I've heard your name before," she said. "Did you go to Marshall?"

You remember people better from high school than you ever can again, first and last names and whole personalities. Part of how much better everything was. I wondered what kind of reputation I had left there that my name would stick in Gabrielle's mind—the girl from the wrong zone? I always thought I had been invisible at Marshall.

Mary thrived on artists and knew all the same ones I did but on a different level. While I tried to exist at the mercy of art directors by doing free-lance art, Mary was the laughing, blond, beautiful dilet-tante who always said the right things, like, "Brilliant, my dear, positively sensational!" as she made her way to one's best work as though drawn by a magnet.

Or, when she looked at the work of a crummy enemy she'd hiss through her teeth, "Oh, the emperor's new clothes, I see . . ."

One night I invited an artist friend over and he brought another artist who brought what looked like a high-fashion model but was really Mary. I was suspicious of her when she first walked in, so tall and blond and of-a-piece, but she was so oblivious to how odd she looked in that black chiffon, sitting on my one-room-apartment floor rolling joints, that who could help just giving up and loving her? She reminded me of a tulip, almost, the way she bent forward at the waist to hand me a lighted joint.

And as they were leaving she leaned close and said she'd tele-phone me soon and that it had been an honor to meet me. A few days later she called to ask me over for coffee.

She was living not too far from the Chateau in one of those hid-den hillside bungalows. It was a beautiful little house, not fancy or expensive but exactly right. Just in front of her place I got a flat tire. Instead of parking in front and going inside and telephoning the Auto Club, I limped two blocks farther and parked. Such was the spell about Mary that you didn't want to clutter up her morning with vulgarities like flats.

When I walked the two blocks back to Mary's she was just put-ting down the phone with a troubled look.

"Mmmm," she said, "that Gabrielle . . . Such luck. Goes away for the weekend and someone breaks in and steals all her jewels."

I was so glad I hadn't mentioned the tire. If you're going to have a problem around Mary, it seemed to me that stolen jewels were the right level.

Pamela told me how her London editor had demanded a story about Gabrielle Sanford because of her current romance with Daniel Wiley, the rumors that they were inseparable, that she might—any day now—change her name to his.

"Did you talk to Mary?" I asked.

"Sanford, you mean? Yes. She gave me quite a good quote, actually. She told me . . . let me see, where're my notes . . . here it is—she said, 'Gabrielle Sanford lives more in a moment than most of us do in a week.' Very printable. She was in New York."

"How'd she look?"

"Who?"

"Mary."

"Mary Sanford." She paused a moment. "Do you know, I can't . . . I can't really say that I noticed. She seemed . . . absent. Vacant. Sad."

I found that I'd been holding my breath.

Women fell in love with Mary. They thought of her as unattainably beautiful and adopted as many of her mannerisms as they could. It didn't matter to them that she lacked that element, raw and beckoning, that trailed like a vapor after Gabrielle. There was an exotic, ladylike essence in Mary that stunned women who understood just what utter waxlike, blossom perfection she was.

I understand that in prison people talk about food first and then sex, with a capacity for detail second to none. I have had discussions with women about Mary, what she wore, what she said, and how she entered . . . We fixed the details forever in our memories.

". . . and the *ring*," one would say, "that lilac opal! Ohhhh! Out of everything, I think that the ring is my favorite."

"No, no," another would say, "it was the eye shadow, the way it just disappeared into her tan. That was the best."

Her manners had been implanted in a French convent where they taught her to write notes of praise and thanks, to say the right thing at funerals and weddings, to send charmingly worded postcards when she was away, and to banish social uneasiness by swift acts of mercy. They taught her to be silent when there was nothing she could do about it.

It was forever fascinating to me that men never noticed much about Mary other than, "Well, I mean, she's pretty and everything . . ."

That high gloss, which floored women, went right over men's heads. It was as though they had no receivers for her particular wavelength. The most you'd ever hear from a man was a general appreciation of how you didn't have to wait an hour for her to get dressed. "By god," an Englishman once told me, "that Mary is not like you others... She just slaps a hat on her head and she's out the door."

The hat would have been the subject of dreamy contemplation with women forever.

"There's just something about Mary," a guy told me once. "She's too pure. She's almost like a nun."

But Mary was much better than nuns. They only came in black and white, while Mary was all the colors.

Gabrielle and Mary were always together, which was odd because Mary knew that most of her friends were not in the mood to see Gabrielle most of the time. It wasn't that Gabrielle actually did much open damage. It was just that the potential was always looming nearby. And women were terrified and hid their lovers when she came in. "Dana had to leave real fast because her father was dying," one girl told me, "and her bed wasn't even cool before Gabrielle was in it with Dana's husband."

"Gabrielle uses Mary," an artist explained to me once.

"For what?" I asked. What did Gabrielle need? I'd decided for myself that Gabrielle wasn't really completely impossible one night when she told me a story and kept me enthralled for an hour. But what would she "use" Mary for?

"She uses Mary to remove . . . to detoxify herself," the artist said. "Gabrielle is much too toxic."

"Well, but isn't that poison bad for Mary?" I asked.

"Of *course*!" he said. "But even Mary likes to play with fire. We all do."

Gabrielle, meanwhile, was assuming all of Mary's outward affectations: her walk, the way she dressed, her speech. She learned how to talk through her teeth and not finish sentences, as though she were too rich and bored to open her mouth or bother with the rest of a thought.

I saw them, the three of them, Gabrielle, Mary, and Edward, one night at a Neil Young opening. Gabrielle's hair was wreathed in gardenias "from the Scorpions..." she mumbled. "The Luau, you know..." (They have huge rum drinks at The Luau in which gardenias float.)

"We've been there since three..." Mary said, "...very festive. Edward and Groucho here"—Gabrielle's pet name was Groucho—"got a divorce. Named me correspondent. We're going to Tana's after this. Come with us."

"No, I'm too old," I said. I was always saying the wrong thing around Mary but I couldn't think of what to say that would have carried the right note of careless worldly sincerity. I was twenty-eight like Mary, Gabrielle was twenty-six, and Edward was thirty-two. I had the right looks but I was always saying the wrong thing. And sometimes, like that evening, I would say such dreadful things that even Mary lost a beat before laughing and pretending she hadn't heard.

"Gabrielle's off for the continent tomorrow," Mary said, changing the subject. "The Grand Tour."

"Yeah," Gabrielle said. "And Mary won't come with me. 'Beaching it,' she says. I told her there'd be an earthquake this summer so she might as well come with me."

"I wouldn't leave L.A. if the whole place tipped over into the ocean," Mary declared. And indeed, she only left Los Angeles on urgent business. She was too tough and too fragile for anyplace else.

I couldn't imagine Gabrielle going without Mary. But she seemed determined. Edward was his normal good-tempered self, taking them all out for drinks after the divorce, ready to foot the bill for any plan.

That summer I came the closest to knowing Mary that I ever would. The awe never diminished, but I learned how to talk so that if I got a flat tire, I could make it amusing enough to park in front of her house. I regarded her basically with the same disbelief that a serf has for the young prince of the manor.

The first time Mary telephoned to see if I wanted to come to the beach with her, I was so shaken that I just sat there thinking about my threadbare bathing suit.

"...are you still there, my dear?" Mary asked. "Of course, I always go to Venice. It's the closest. No crowds. Dr. Laszlo says this is my last summer in the sun, my skin really shouldn't be out there at all."

Maybe it was because I was both a woman and an artist that Mary affected me the way she did, I don't know. But I just could not imagine Mary going to the beach like an ordinary person.

Venice that summer looked like a Hopper painting. American vistas of shadow and light on the sides of slatted buildings through a whitish mist. Occasionally an airplane would drone out over the Pacific before looping back to fly east. And there was Mary, lying on the sand like an ordinary person only better, because without her makeup she almost looked ordinary and it was secret, like having the *Mona Lisa* in the trunk of your car without the frame. I didn't feel ordinary.

"Mmmmmm..." Mary would say, after fifteen minutes, "I feel like I've died..."

I looked over anxiously the first time.

"...and gone to heaven," she concluded. "And now *this* has to come up."

Slightly annoyed, Mary told me that when she got home from the beach she'd have to shower and go to a charity tea that one of the Sanfords was in charge of because a month before she'd offered to "pour."

It was those kind of details that made me feel awkward, those combined with Mary being so effortlessly slender and blond and tall. We all knew, of course, that she lightened her hair, but the women knew that she just did that to enhance her ethereal position. The guy who lived in a bungalow next to hers once told me that he always thought of Mary as the "girl next door." "Just an ordinary girl," he insisted. "I just don't understand why you women think she's so fucking special—my girlfriend can't get over her... She's just the girl next door."

Gabrielle was in Morocco eating milk and honey and opium in

the well-gossiped-about company of a French movie director. With Gabrielle away, Mary seemed easier, more gentle, and I thought that if she were left to her own devices, she would become one of those Pilgrim virgins from Nathaniel Hawthorne who went around casting sunbeams into the hearts of all who beheld them. When Gabrielle was around, a sarcastic streak glittered through Mary's conversation, though Mary's was a pale reflection of Gabrielle's toxic irony.

But that summer when we went often to the beach, Mary reminded me of a sweet prince in exile waking up on Easter. She was so light.

When I said that men didn't look at Mary the way women did, this didn't mean that Mary was not the most popular girl. She was constantly engaged in romances, her phone always rang, and she even had a couple of what Joyce Haber called "dates" with Cary Grant. ("Actually," she told me, "we didn't go *out*." I was too numbed to ask if they'd never been together or if they'd just stayed home.)

Her bungalow was always bustling with suitcases in the little informal front porch/foyer and the men that passed through her living room and out to the zinnia garden were usually newly famous and all the rage. I sometimes thought that Mary was what you got—your reward—for reaching the top and being young, rich, and handsome. Beatles and movie stars, writers and country singers, and of course always her L.A. artists, who were the most fun of all. Ed Ruscha, Billy Al Bengston, Larry Bell, Ken Price, and Ed Moses all gave her wonderful pieces small enough to fit in her house. Sometimes late at night through some invisible chemistry of Mary's, new friendships would be formed between unlikely combinations, and unlike Mme Verdurin, Mary never tried to hold on to people. If you met someone at Mary's or through Mary (she was simplicity itself at irresistible introductions, saying, "This is Archie Lowencliff, my darling, you remember, Michael's friend who does those marvelous blue sculptures you died over..."), you didn't have to give her ten percent of the friendship. And Mary would sit on the arm of her couch, unconsciously weaving her delicate feet into impossible postures, her head leaning forward to listen with a dreamy contentment in her face, her hands forgotten except for a joint hanging limply from her fingers. She was a major social instigator, a force for parties. Her two special words were "festive" and "perfect." And throughout it all, she remained true to her convent manner; there were always the phone calls the next morning with her kind, sleepy, yawning, "You were wonderful last night, my dear. I don't know how you do it; your dinners are always perfect. You are a little rascal in the kitchen, aren't you?"

She did not wear fur or eat meat. One time a grand-dame lady came to town and wanted to eat greasy spareribs the minute she got off the plane (she'd been in Paris for too long). Mary brought me along to provide an excuse in case she couldn't stand it, because Mary was not a good liar and I am a great one. I sat and watched Mary turn greener and greener as the bones piled up in front of her. Her grilled-cheese sandwich had grown cold. Finally I said, "Oh dear, I forgot I have to meet my sister in fifteen minutes and my car's . . ." And we ran out into the rain, and Mary sat behind her steering wheel for five minutes without starting the motor, breathing deeply, with her eyes closed, regaining what Jane Austen used to call "composure."

"Those bones . . ." she sighed at last, released.

When her cat got run over she mourned for a week.

Mary told me once that eventually she imagined she'd live at the beach, and I knew she meant that eventually she would marry one of her rich, handsome men and go live happily ever after by the sea. And desert us. I was frightened and said, "But what about"—I waved my hand to indicate her living room—"all of this?"

"It comes with me," she said. "Everything."

I was still afraid that she would abandon us, but she had promised to take everything so maybe it was all right.

Another guy told me once, "She was just another high-class groupie; she was cold. I never could imagine her in bed with anyone."


Women want to be loved like roses. They spend hours perfecting their eyebrows and toes and inventing irresistible curls that fall by accident down the back of their necks from otherwise austere hair-dos. They want their lover to remember the way they held a glass. They want to haunt.

Men don't work like that as far as I've been able to judge. Men aren't haunted by the way a woman holds a glass. Men are haunted by women who're just like the one who married dear old dad. ("He can't possibly be serious; she's too fat!" one overhears, only to remember that his mother is too fat.) Or else they love a woman because they think she is absolutely unlike their mother and is such an affront to everything their mother stands for that it will plague her for the rest of her life. One time I knew an angelic-looking nineteen-year-old boy whose mother was a Las Vegas showgirl even at the age of thirty-six. And this kid found himself a thirty-year-old girlfriend who wore glasses and no make-up. His mother was so furious she drove her car into his girlfriend's apartment. The only time men fall in love with roses is on douche commercials.

Anthony Sutter came to L.A. to open a branch of the family Wall Street firm on the West Coast, and Mary met him at the charity tea where she'd been pouring. He was thirty-five and divorced and crisply Harvard. He had an East Coast grasp of the situation that was at odds with the pace of L.A., and he wore ties, even on weekends. He was handsome, and by the time I got to meet him, he and Mary seemed to have arrived at an understanding: It was as though all at once Mary wasn't there.

"Well, who *is* he?" I asked, the first time I saw Mary with this glazed expression.

"Money," Mary said.

Pamela looked over her green steno notes and said, "That's what I mean about you people out here. Your *attitudes*! Saying you don't know what love means!"

"With them," I said, "I'm confused."

"About love . . . I don't believe it. But that's not the only thing. It's everyone's attitude about money as well. When I went to interview

Daniel Wiley and Gabrielle they were living on the floor! No furniture. I know he's a millionaire. Why are they sleeping on the floor?"

"He's making deals," I said. "Anyway, movie people don't need furniture."

"Not even a bed!?"

Daniel Wiley is starring Gabrielle in his next movie. She plays a murderess; she'll be perfect. They've forgotten about beds, and I understand, because once you set sail on a movie, you are out of touch with ordinary land. Movie-makers between movies seem like you and me; they go to parties, they shop, they swim. But they're just treading water, waiting for another injection, another ship to come take them away in film. And money has nothing to do with it.

"Gabrielle told me that she's in love for the first time," Pamela said. "And it must be love or she wouldn't be sleeping on the floor. Or would she?"

I first saw Daniel Wiley fifteen years ago at Barney's Beanery. He was wired for ambition; everything else about him was weak and silly except for his sheer, unswerving Hollywood belief that he, more than anyone, knew what movies were. He never said much, but he had his eyes continually peripheral, noticing the whole row of pinball machines and not just his own. And so nine years ago, when he took over an about-to-be-abandoned movie and charged it up with everything he knew, it took off across the country and made a mint. When I first saw him fresh from Texas and he told me in all seriousness that he wanted women screaming after him in the way they did for the Beatles, I told him he was crazy and that no one went to the movies anymore.

"They will now," he said. "I'm here."

Gabrielle had always believed in movies too. It drew them together.

I once ran into Mary in the parking lot of the Arrow Market on Santa Monica.

"Your hair!" I cried. I hadn't seen her in a long time and now her hair was an ordinary brown. She was dressed in jeans and an old red pullover and loafers, and her hair was in a pony tail and she had no make-up on so you could hardly see her.

"It was falling out, my dear"—her voice was dull—"from all that bleach."

I didn't believe it.

"Are you still with that Anthony Sutter?"

"He's all I do anymore," she yawned.

"How's Gabrielle?"

"I don't see that much of her. He doesn't like her."

"But she's..." I felt betrayed. If Mary was willing to give up Gabrielle, then she could give everything up, all of us. And for what? What kind of money was this East Coast money where you couldn't even see your friends? What did he want Mary to be?

"How much money," I asked, "does he have, anyway?"

But it wasn't just the money. I knew it couldn't be just money. It was that she was afraid of getting old without living out a girlhood fantasy of one day marrying and having children and a house and a business-husband. She had always been conventional, that was what was so great about her. She was almost thirty. I had thought about it myself; getting married and calling it a day, but then, after San Francisco, I knew those songs of love were not for me. There was very little precedent for not getting married, I'll admit, and the women I knew who weren't were all going to analysts and wondering what was the matter with themselves. But if Mary wanted to get married, then I would have to think seriously about it because Mary always knew when to do things and how. So now, suddenly, she wasn't doing clothes anymore and she was closing up her petals. I felt cold in the Arrow Market parking lot, looking at Mary's plain face and ordinary hair and sensible clothes. Did it mean that we were going to have to be gloomy now that we were about to be thirty? Or maybe she was in love with him and it ate up all her charm.

Her nervous charm and beauty had been so easily banished it made you afraid for beauty itself.

So there I was, putting my groceries in the back of the car, waving good-bye to Mary. Alone in the twilight outside the Arrow Market, all at once not knowing, at the age of twenty-nine, what any of the main givens were: love, money, or beauty. To say nothing of truth, of course.

It was three years before Pamela's that I'd gone over for a drink at a friend's at the Chateau, and forty-eight hours later the elevator doors opened out to the basement parking lot where I had thoughtlessly parked, telling the attendant I'd only be a minute. I was fumbling for my sunglasses when I bumped right into Gabrielle and Mary coming across the driveway from the pool. They were dressed in their bathing suits, carried towels, glasses, and Mary held a large Thermos.

"I thought you..." I said, looking at Mary. She was light as a feather and had that slight streak of sarcasm that always opened up in her when she was around Gabrielle, that cruel tinge to her laughter that of course no business-husband would approve of. There was the same worldly, familiar quality of flat judgments and sophisticated hilarious remarks. Even her physical posture wasn't what you'd call a modest womanly virtue. Virtue was not an issue.

"My dear," she said, "come have a drink."

"He's out of town," Gabrielle said, "for a whole weekend."

"Oh, goody," I said, backing back into the elevator.

"You must see what Groucho brought me from Oslo," Mary said.

"What have you guys been doing?" I asked. I felt surprisingly comfortable being with them, as though I didn't have to explain anything or get through the usual walls of misunderstanding that I did with most people in those days who were worried about my "future" and why wasn't I married. We are shy in Hollywood about discussing concrete realities like the future. "I haven't seen you in a year, Gabrielle. You look wonderful."

"We've been drinking," Mary said, stepping out on the fourth floor where the elevator stopped, "since yesterday morning."

"Tequila," Gabrielle said. "Among other things."

"Too bad you missed Carl," Mary said. Carl, like Gabrielle, was one of those people a business-husband would never tolerate. He always wore white and men loathed him.

"What's Carl doing nowadays?" I asked.

"Producing," Gabrielle said, unlocking the door of a two-bedroom suite. "Come see what else I got."

The apartment looked out to the southwest; you could see the ocean, and it was so clear it looked like a glass ribbon. (There were fires to compensate in Ventura County. It's hard to have a clear day in L.A. without those fiery winds.) It was a stock, unpersonalized Chateau suite, except for Gabrielle's clothes and some open suitcases and a toothbrush and toothpaste in the bathroom. Gabrielle never wore make-up or perfume or did anything like that, although for years Mary had tried to convince her about Laszlo, and finally Gabrielle had gone down to Saks, gotten the bottles, listened to the instructions, and lost everything on her way to the parking lot.

"Regardez, my petite chou," Gabrielle said, opening a drawer of the telephone stand and revealing a mirror with an inch-high mountain of white crystals. "Cocaine. Le cocaine pure."

"Have a drink first," Mary said, vanishing into the kitchen. Gabrielle opened a brown glass bottle and touched her finger to the top, so a small wet spot was evident. When my drink arrived, Gabrielle said, "Here," and dipped her finger into it, and then she returned so quickly to the cocaine that I became absorbed and forgetful and coked.

"Take that off," Gabrielle said to me, looking at what I was wearing. "You'll be much more comfortable in this."

She handed me a Finnish cotton kaftan and there I was, out of my clothes again, the way I had been (for two days on another floor) only an hour before. Mary and Gabrielle both wore kaftans too. Gabrielle's was wrinkled and had had red wine or blood spilled down the side and Mary's was perfect, freshly laundered and light. Mary leaned against the French window, looked out toward Catalina with an expression of her old dreamy contentment upon her once-again ravishing face. I knew now why she'd looked so ordinary in the Arrow Market: She was trying to look ordinary.

"I'm trying to convince this one to come to Rio with me," Gabrielle said in a low voice about Mary, who was too far away to hear. "Carnival!"

"But Mary'll never..." I began. My mouth tasted rusty like blood and I felt a wave of invincible elation cresting in white foam. It couldn't have been the coke. "What was that on your finger, Gabrielle?"

"What?" she asked, frowning. "Oh, the drink. Sandoz, my dear, all the way from the mountains of Switzerland. Le LSD pour les jeunes filles."

"You're not going to talk French the whole time, are you?" I asked. "Was it a lot?"

"Enough, probably," she answered.

"But you guys are taking cocaine on acid?" I wondered. How could they remember to take cocaine when they were in Eden? I was grateful to be wearing just loose cotton as the afternoon got underway.

We laughed for four hours. Mary kept pouring herself more tequila in a glass tumbler all the way to the top. Every time I tried to rise up from the couch I fell back down again laughing. Gabrielle ran things.

At dusk Gabrielle sat on the floor with her elbows on the coffee table, waiting for us to quiet down so she could begin.

"I told you about the Coyote's Brain, didn't I? I didn't? Odd. I haven't told anyone about the Coyote's Brain, but I *must* have told you... Are you sure not? Well...

"Jean-Paul and I were in Tangiers, we'd been in Morocco for about a month, and it seemed to me that everywhere we went I'd hear about this stuff called Coyote's Brain. The women talked about it, but if you asked a man he'd just clam up. But one night, this woman who happened to speak English told me that among the locals there was this superstition that if you had a white powder called Coyote's Brain and wore it in this silver jar around your neck... well, it's hard to describe, but everything about you would be intensified. Everything.

"So naturally I asked her where I could get some and she acted like I was crazy or something and said, '*We* Europeans don't believe such silly things.'"

Gabrielle paused. She peered out the window at the lighted city. It was one of those warm nights, like the night I first saw her grown up at her party. You could hear the Sunset Strip cars below and the rock and roll next door. She shot her eyes back to the coffee table in front of her, where her hands were lying calmly, and continued.

"So the *next* night, we went out with this French anthropologist who was doing research on things like witchcraft and I asked *him* where I could get some Coyote's Brain.

"'How many living grandmothers do you have?' he asked me, and I said, 'Two,' so he said, 'Well, tomorrow morning someone will come to pick up the money, which you are to divide up equally into two envelopes or containers.' I asked, 'Well, how much?' and he said, 'As much as you think it's worth. But do not divulge the amount to anyone ever.'

"And the next day, this little girl, she must have been about ten, comes to my door in the morning... She had a ring through her nose and black around her eyes and she was wearing mostly pink and green and I handed her the envelopes."

"How much did you give her?" Mary asked.

"I can't say. I told you I couldn't say. The guy told me not to tell anyone... I'll say this one thing though, just this one."

She looked up from the table into our waiting faces and she smiled like a ten-year-old herself.

"I gave her all I had."

I winced from a knock on the door. A loud, angry knock like it was the police or something, and then the door opened and it was Anthony.

"Darling!" Mary said, on her feet and rushing to him.

"I thought you told me you weren't going to see her anymore," he said icily, looking at Gabrielle with hate.

"But darling, we're just..."

"She's not..." I said.

"You promised you wouldn't!" he said.

Gabrielle picked up a deck of cards and began to lay out a hand of solitaire on the coffee table, frowning.

"But I..." Mary doubled over and began to gag. She fled into the bathroom, where we could hear her throwing up.

"Go see how she is," Gabrielle told me. I looked back and forth at the two of them, wondering if it was safe. "Go!" Gabrielle said, so I went.

Mary was curled over like an arch from whose mouth a gorgeous waterfall of yellow spurted. Tears were rolling down her cheeks and into the toilet too, and she was helpless.

I could hear faint voices from the other room and then a door slammed.

Mary gasped and sank down on her knees against the bathtub, sobbing herself back together.

I left her there and went into the living room, where Gabrielle was still sitting on the floor playing solitaire on the coffee table.

"He's gone?"

"Yes," she said.

"Did you get it?"

"What? Oh, the Coyote's Brain? I...What do you think?"

"I think I better go home," I said. It was next to impossible getting out of the parking lot in that condition, and I was still wearing Gabrielle's kaftan.


If I live to be a hundred, I don't think I'll ever be unable to summon up Mary's wistful baby voice, so placating and hopeless as she rushed up to Anthony saying, "Darling..."

His face was hard, icy and vengeful. But he wasn't aiming at Mary, whom he didn't seem to notice even when he spoke to her, since his eyes were locked into Gabrielle's ponds of innocence. I wondered afterward how he knew Mary was there or if Gabrielle had created the whole thing. Mary had been the object of a war between ordinary solid American values and Hollywood, where even money is lost in the shuffle among the hard floors and 5:00 a.m. wardrobe calls of an invisible city named for a plant that never existed, named by a clan that waits for the next movie to sail away on.

A woman I know who's been business manager of a national magazine for years, and is still young, took stock of her life and decided that even if she made half as much money, she would rather be a story editor in Hollywood than hold her present executive position. She asked me if I could help her and I thought about it and called around. Carl said, "She just has to have one thing."

"What?" I asked.

"A father in the industry."

To get in, you have to be born in or start at twenty like Daniel or Gabrielle. Or marry in, although others don't like that—pushy wives and husbands are not suffered gladly.

I had never thought about what it took to get out, though. Mary had tried to get out, to join the mortals, to change her name. It robbed her of her style; she became, as Pamela intimated, invisible. She accompanied Gabrielle to Rio, but she didn't come back after. She stayed traveling; she went everywhere but Hollywood. Carl saw her in Hawaii having Zombies at the Royal Hawaiian Bar awhile ago and he told me that Mary had "lost her looks."

"You don't say things like 'lost her looks,'" I said. "Is she getting wrinkles or what?"

"It's something from inside," Carl said. "She's so thin. It's as though she's caving in; her rib cage is like a bird's. She's still gorgeous. She was wearing some kind of faded-rose suede suit that really must have been beautiful. But when I thought about her afterward, I couldn't figure out why she *did* it anymore. Why she did it at all."

The awkward basement pillars of the Chateau Marmont support the past. The ghosts and furies from Alla Nazimova's garden eventually wafted across Sunset when the respectable savings and loan building was erected by Bart Lytton. He probably thought that he could just come and build and the Garden would cease, but a few years later he lost everything, and not long after that, despondent, he killed himself. That's the trouble with Hollywood; the things that don't exist are likely to kill you if you threaten them. His personality died with him, and now the place has no style; it's been renamed from Lytton Savings to Great Western, and it's utterly bland, a neuter. A little model of the Garden of Allah is out front for curious tourists to see how it was.

It must have been marvelous when the century was young and things impressed themselves in such blatant vivid brilliance that an approaching fire under a starry sky could illuminate, even to a Crimean actress, this sense of "place"—that there was nothing to be wanted from material things, nothing to be saved.

# TITLES IN SERIES

*For a complete list of titles, visit www.nyrb.com or write to:*
*Catalog Requests, NYRB, 435 Hudson Street, New York, NY 10014*

* *Also available as an electronic book.*

**G.B. EDWARDS** The Book of Ebenezer Le Page*

**JOHN EHLE** The Land Breakers*

**MARCELLUS EMANTS** A Posthumous Confession

**EURIPIDES** Grief Lessons: Four Plays; translated by Anne Carson

**J.G. FARRELL** Troubles*

**J.G. FARRELL** The Siege of Krishnapur*

**J.G. FARRELL** The Singapore Grip*

**ELIZA FAY** Original Letters from India

**KENNETH FEARING** The Big Clock

**KENNETH FEARING** Clark Gifford's Body

**FÉLIX FÉNÉON** Novels in Three Lines*

**M.I. FINLEY** The World of Odysseus

**THOMAS FLANAGAN** The Year of the French*

**BENJAMIN FONDANE** Existential Monday: Philosophical Essays*

**SANFORD FRIEDMAN** Conversations with Beethoven*

**SANFORD FRIEDMAN** Totempole*

**MASANOBU FUKUOKA** The One-Straw Revolution*

**MARC FUMAROLI** When the World Spoke French

**CARLO EMILIO GADDA** That Awful Mess on the Via Merulana

**BENITO PÉREZ GÁLDOS** Tristana*

**MAVIS GALLANT** The Cost of Living: Early and Uncollected Stories*

**MAVIS GALLANT** Paris Stories*

**MAVIS GALLANT** A Fairly Good Time *with* Green Water, Green Sky*

**MAVIS GALLANT** Varieties of Exile*

**GABRIEL GARCÍA MÁRQUEZ** Clandestine in Chile: The Adventures of Miguel Littín

**LEONARD GARDNER** Fat City*

**ALAN GARNER** Red Shift*

**WILLIAM H. GASS** In the Heart of the Heart of the Country: And Other Stories*

**WILLIAM H. GASS** On Being Blue: A Philosophical Inquiry*

**THÉOPHILE GAUTIER** My Fantoms

**JEAN GENET** Prisoner of Love

**ÉLISABETH GILLE** The Mirador: Dreamed Memories of Irène Némirovsky by Her Daughter*

**JEAN GIONO** Hill*

**JOHN GLASSCO** Memoirs of Montparnasse*

**P.V. GLOB** The Bog People: Iron-Age Man Preserved

**NIKOLAI GOGOL** Dead Souls*

**EDMOND AND JULES DE GONCOURT** Pages from the Goncourt Journals

**PAUL GOODMAN** Growing Up Absurd: Problems of Youth in the Organized Society*

**EDWARD GOREY (EDITOR)** The Haunted Looking Glass

**JEREMIAS GOTTHELF** The Black Spider*

**A.C. GRAHAM** Poems of the Late T'ang

**WILLIAM LINDSAY GRESHAM** Nightmare Alley*

**HANS HERBERT GRIMM** Schlump*

**EMMETT GROGAN** Ringolevio: A Life Played for Keeps

**VASILY GROSSMAN** An Armenian Sketchbook*

**VASILY GROSSMAN** Everything Flows*

**VASILY GROSSMAN** Life and Fate*

**VASILY GROSSMAN** The Road*

**OAKLEY HALL** Warlock

**PATRICK HAMILTON** The Slaves of Solitude*

**PATRICK HAMILTON** Twenty Thousand Streets Under the Sky*

**PETER HANDKE** Short Letter, Long Farewell

**PETER HANDKE** Slow Homecoming